KU-162-724

PENGUIN BOOKS

CHARLOTTE'S ROW

H. E. Bates was born in 1905 at Rushden in Northampton-
shire, and was educated at Kettering Grammar School. He
worked as a journalist and clerk on a local newspaper before
publishing his first book, *The Two Sisters*, when he was
twenty. In the next fifteen years he acquired a distinguished
reputation for his stories about English country life. During
the Second World War he was a Squadron Leader in the
RAF and some of his stories of service life, *The Greatest
People in the World* (1942), *How Sleep the Brave* (1943) and
The Face of England (1953), were written under the pseudo-
nym of 'Flying Officer X'. His subsequent novels of Burma,
The Purple Plain and *The Jacaranda Tree*, and of India, *The
Scarlet Sword*, stemmed directly or indirectly from his war
experience in the Eastern theatre of war.

In 1958 his writing took a new direction with the appearance
of *The Darling Buds of May*, the first of the popular Larkin
family novels, which was followed by *A Breath of French Air*,
When the Green Woods Laugh, *Oh! To Be in England* (1963)
and *A Little of What You Fancy* (1970). His autobiography
appeared in three volumes, *The Vanished World* (1960), *The
Blossoming World* (1971) and *The World in Ripeness* (1972).
His last works included a novel, *The Triple Echo* (1971), and
a collection of short stories, *The Song of the Wren* (1972).
Perhaps one of his most famous works of fiction is the best-
selling novel *Fair Stood the Wind for France* (1944). H. E.
Bates also wrote miscellaneous works on gardening, essays
on country life, several plays including *The Day of Glory*
(1945), *The Modern Short Story* (1941) and a story for children, *The White Admiral* (1968). His works have been trans-
lated into sixteen languages and a posthumous collection of
his stories, *The Yellow Meads of Asphodel*, appeared in 1976.

H. E. Bates was awarded the CBE in 1973 and died in
January 1974. He was married in 1931 and had four children.

H. E. BATES

CHARLOTTE'S ROW

PENGUIN BOOKS

H. E. BATES

CHARLOTTE'S ROW

PENGUIN BOOKS

Penguin Books Ltd, Harmondsworth, Middlesex, England
Viking Penguin Inc., 40 West 23rd Street, New York, New York 10010, U.S.A.
Penguin Books Australia Ltd, Ringwood, Victoria, Australia
Penguin Books Canada Ltd, 2801 John Street, Markham, Ontario, Canada L3R 1B4
Penguin Books (N.Z.) Ltd, 182–190 Wairau Road, Auckland 10, New Zealand

First published by Jonathan Cape 1931
Published in Penguin Books 1987

Made and printed in Great Britain by
Richard Clay Ltd, Bungay, Suffolk
Typeset in Times

To
HENRY JAMES BYROM

CHARLOTTE'S ROW

CHAPTER I

QUINTUS JABEZ HARPER had carried on a business as a
shoemaker at number seventeen Charlotte's Row for
twenty years. He was a good craftsman when he could per-
suade himself to work between his bouts of heavy drinking,
his very gay visits to the races and the mysterious expeditions on which he sometimes took with him a pair of light
yellow ferrets, sometimes a little white terrier, and sometimes two handsome great harriers that were a soft, beautiful fawn-colour, like deer. His poaching expeditions were
very successful. He rarely returned without a rabbit and
there had often been occasions when the family had tasted
pheasant on Sundays. But he lost what he won at racing
and for twenty years the Harpers had been notorious for
their slipshod, haphazard way of living, always in debt,
eternally dependent on credit, borrowings which were
never repaid, and on weekly visits to a Jewish pawnbroker
living in the same neighbourhood. Mrs. Harper was a
thrifty, courageous mouse of a woman. The shoemaker, in
his drunken fits, often floored her with one hand as easily
as he could overbalance a little pepper-pot with one finger.
They were both a little over fifty. Quintus was still a
healthy black-headed giant who carried himself with a
swaggering air, his powerful shoulders drawn boldly back,
his arms dangling wide and loose like a negro's, his head
thrust forward on its thick red neck in an aggressive
fashion, rather like that of a boxer. His face was strongly
modelled; the lips were red and thick and proud, the eyes
black and arrogantly handsome except when sullen and
red with drinking. His whole body was heavily muscled

9

and his chest was covered with a thickness of black hair like a pelt. He was coarse, proud, swaggering, indolent. He despised religion and as a socialist was pugilistically impatient to accomplish the revolution. He sneered at weakness; his god was strength and his passions were beer and revolution. When he worked at the bench he was forced to wear a pair of black-rimmed spectacles, which he tied behind his ears with a piece of wax-string. As a sign of physical weakness he hated them, suffering them with great disgust and peering over them with muttered curses. They gave him an amusing, less terrifying air and an odd, squinting expression in which there lurked something racily humorous and faintly diabolical.

He came out of his shop soon after six one April evening and went into Charlotte's Row carrying a bundle of boots on his shoulder. Easter was very near and the sky was a pale, cold green, as if with coming frost. Charlotte's Row was composed of two rows of dark yellowish brick houses which sloped gently downwards towards a railway-arch spanning the lower end; the houses were small, dark and poverty-stricken, with regular holes of entry to backyards, like a line of kennels. At one end they were shut in by a tall brick wall that was like the wall of a prison. A railway-engine was shunting backwards and forwards over the railway-bridge, making melancholy shrieks that echoed for a long time over the dark town spreading beyond. A close, pestilential stench hung over the row, a smell of humanity living in a congested space, a stale odour of cooking and rotting filth, a breath of leather from a boot-factory, a musty, powerful smell of malt from a brewery standing on the bank of the canal beyond the railway-arch, a stench of smoke, poverty and sordid living. It was not dark enough for the street lamps to be alight, but there were already lights in the beer-house on the street corner, and a fan-shaped flame of orange and blue gaslight in the bake-

10

house facing it. The door of the beer-house was standing open and the white handles of the beer-engines and the coloured labels of the bottles stood out clearly in the gloom. Beyond the narrow windows of the bakehouse the gigantic shadow of the baker would roam slowly at intervals, blackening the white walls. The baker was a Strict and Particular Baptist, and the following day would be Good Friday. The baker would make many hundreds of buns, but afraid of committing profanity and believing in a special heaven for himself, he would take care that none of his buns bore the mark of the Cross. Gradually the sky changed from green to blue and presently the railway-engine clanked out of the distance, thundered over the dark bridge and passed away.

A small boy of nine or ten had been sitting for a long time on the steps of the bakery. Occasionally, standing on tip-toe, he would try to peer in at the bakehouse window, but he was not tall enough to see anything but the topmost oven, long shelves filled with blocks of salt and the peels lying on the racks under the ceiling. He was anxious to ask the baker if he needed help on Good Friday but at the sight of the shadow roaming across the walls he was curiously afraid, imagining that the baker was about to rush out and beat him.

When he sat on the steps again and watched the fading spring sky and listened to the railway-engine his face assumed a pensive, watchful air. He was very thin, his cheeks distinctly hollow, his legs like frail sticks peeled of their bark. His hair, the colour of ripened barley, lay almost hidden beneath a black cap with a very wide peak, on which he had pinned a coloured miniature of a brigadier set in a gilded frame. His eyes were astonishingly blue and lay deep in his head, so that their colour was darkened and their expression filled with dreaminess. He looked altogether frail and nervous and sometimes his mouth and eyes worked with a curious agitation, as if he were half-afraid of being pounced upon unexpectedly.

The shoemaker began to call the boy's name with powerful shouts as he was about to peer into the bakehouse again. The boy started at once, slipped quickly off the stone step and stood upright, glancing about him.

The shoemaker made impatient signals with his hand, shouting:

'Adam! Adam!'

In reply the boy began to walk slowly, as if reluctantly, up the street, the shoemaker still calling him powerfully by his name:

'Adam! Adam! Adam!'

The shoemaker was wearing a long black apron; a very dirty shirt was rolled up to his elbows, his forearms showing big, thick, black and hairy. Besides the boots he was holding an oil-can in his hands.

As the boy approached he began to walk towards him with long strides, swaggering from side to side with a heavy movement of his shoulders, and when the boy was still fifty yards away he spoke.

He spoke in a voice of tremendous depth, and the sound of his voice and his gigantic frame seemed to exaggerate the pale, fragile appearance of the boy.

'Will you go with the shoes to Daniel's?' he boomed. 'Sewn and stitched. You can remember that, four pair sewn and stitched, can't you? They'll know. Can you match it if I sling them on your shoulder?'

And suddenly the boots were slung across the boy's back before he could move or reply. He staggered a little under the weight of them and the shoemaker put the oil-can into his hands.

'And call in at Masher Jonathan's for a pint of oil,' he said.

The boy stood for a moment perfectly still, in hesitation,

12

as if still waiting for something. The shoemaker, who had turned away, turned back again, and seeing him, boomed out:

'Oh, Masher'll let you have it on tick.'

At these words the boy at once turned, and stooping a little under the weight of the boots, began to walk down the street. The words had relieved him. He remembered another occasion when he had gone to Masher's for oil for the shoemaker and Mrs. Jonathan had given him a message. 'Tell him,' she had said vehemently, 'from me, to burn a little beer in his bloody lamp until he's wiped his slate here.' And when in his simplicity the boy had returned to deliver these instructions, the shoemaker had flown into a rage and boxed his ears. Afterwards, however, a curious scene had taken place in Masher's; the shoemaker, entering the shop stormily, had pelted Mrs. Jonathan with money, a penny at a time, flinging the coins into her face like peas, with all his strength, until she had fallen on her knees in order to snatch them up with greedy fingers, bitterly cursing and crying. Ever since that time Mrs. Jonathan had treated the boy with suspicion, and sometimes with contempt, so that he hated going there.

He passed under the railway-bridge and walked along the bank of the canal beyond. The water, motionless and black beneath him, gleamed softly like oil. The lights of the brewery shone distantly on the far bank and there was a faint hum of machinery from the boot-factory farther on. The narrow oblong windows were yellow with light and on them the shadows of machinery loomed enormously, wheels, shaftings and presses working with incessant din. Presses thundered on the blocks with a sound like distant gunfire, wheels kept up a diabolical moaning and chattering, and there was a machine which shrieked and whined like a dying pig.

It was very difficult to carry the boots; his shoulders

13

were cut by the strings and the weight seemed to pull open his mouth, leaving him perpetually gasping and suffering. Figures began to pass him, but they were mere shadows to him, their faces still the familiar faces of poverty. The lower street, smelling strongly of canal-water and leather, was dark except for the lights in Jonathan's at the far end.

After pausing to look at the jars of sweets and a plate of stale sausages in the window he went into the shop. A woman was crouching over the counter, working out some figures with a yellow pencil on a scrap of paper. She did not raise her head but made a curious little nodding sign that she knew he had entered.

'A pint of oil, please,' he said.

Instantly, without raising her head, the woman asked:

'Do you know what time it is?'

Her voice was cold and sharp and the boy stood silent.

'Don't you have clocks in your part of the world?' she said.

He was afraid, and again he did not speak. She had not yet raised her head.

'You see it's dark though, don't you?' she said.

'Yes,' he answered.

Still without raising her head she burst out:

'Don't you know that if I sell oil to people after it's dark I go to gaol and live on bread and water?'

The harshness of the words terrified him. Suddenly she raised her narrow, avaricious face to him, the carmine spots on the cheeks flaming and the large yellow teeth protruding stupidly.

'And that when I come out again I'll have no home to go to, and no money, and no shop, and have to end my days in the workhouse? You don't want me to end my days in the workhouse, do you?'

The boy did not reply. At that moment there was a sud-

14

den hissing from the room behind the shop and a strong odour of frying herrings filled the air.

'And anyway,' Mrs. Jonathan went on, 'who wants oil at this time of night? Not your grandmother?'

'No,' he said guardedly.

'Who then?'

'Quintus Harper.'

Her face assumed at once a look of angry contempt and her voice rose to a bitter snarl.

'Harper? The swine!' she burst out. 'God! So it's Harper? There's two pound six and ten down to him now, I don't know whether he knows it, and now he's got the neck to send you for oil after dark. He knows I could get time for it as easy as snuff. I try to be honest, but if I let you have that oil a policeman would walk in the door, sure enough, before you could lift your little finger. No! I daren't let you have it! No, it's more than I dare do!'

Unexpectedly, as she finished, a voice of quiet, entreating, faintly bitter tones came from behind the shop, startling both the woman and the boy.

'For Christ's sake,' it said, 'for Christ's sake give the boy the oil and shut your mouth.'

In another moment the boy saw the curtain across the doorway pushed back and the speaker himself appear. He stood in his shirt sleeves, with a frying-pan in one hand and a book in the other, and he fixed on Mrs. Jonathan with an expression of half-weary, half-angry bitterness. His small knotty frame and the taciturn face under the thin dark hair burned with vitality; there was something arresting and challenging about the soft jet eyes set without a flicker, the thoughtful forehead, and the sensitive line of the mouth thinned by years of physical toil.

'I said give the boy the oil and let him go,' he said quietly. 'Can't you see that he's going to Daniel's for Quintus? He'll break in half, poor devil, while you stand

15

jawing about your workhouse and your prison. Give him the oil I tell you! Quick!'

'And suppose the police see him?' she flashed round. 'And they ask where he got the oil and he tells them and I get time, what then?'

'If you got time,' he began bitterly, '—well, never mind about that. You give him the oil before I give it him myself.'

'I won't let him have it,' she shrieked. 'I won't let him have it for nobody! I'm damned if I do!'

Calmly and swiftly, Masher Jonathan darted forward, banged down the frying-pan on the counter, leaned over and snatched the can from Adam's hand. The sight of the half-cooked fish still lying in the pan as it stood on the counter fascinated the boy, and the can was taken from him and was being filled somewhere in the dark regions behind before he could look up. Screaming with rage, Mrs. Jonathan ran after Masher and began beating his bent head with her fists, and Adam caught also the sound of dull thuds, as if she were kicking him.

'I'm damned if you shall! There's two pound six and tenpence down to him now. I'm damned if you shall!'

'He's a pal of mine! Get out!'

A smell of spilled paraffin mingled with the odour of fried herring, and Masher came hastily into the shop dragging his wife by the wrist.

'For Christ's sake! You're hurting me! You're killing me!' she raged. She began to beat his breast furiously with her free hand, twisting like a snake and weeping with rage.

'If I wanted to kill you I should chose your neck, not your wrist!'

'Then take it!' she screamed. 'Put your hands on my neck, you dirty swine!'

'Get out! I wouldn't soil myself!'

16

'Take it, take it! I put it under your nose and you daren't touch it!'

'I wouldn't soil myself.'

'Damn you! —interfering pig! —damn you!'

Suddenly she spat at him, and Masher, swinging the oil-can high into the air, as though to strike her, brought it down on the counter with a blow that made the weights jump like fish in the brass scales. A tin of snuff and a piece of cheese flew off the counter. A spasm of hatred possessed Masher's face that made him formidable and terrible; his eyes seemed to have grown blacker and more intense and his fingers gripped the oil-can with passionate ferocity, as if he hated that also.

The boy, filled with awe and expecting that every moment the fish would go flying too, a thing which to him would have been more terrible than all the rest, retreated to the door.

'You run along with the shoes and the oil'll be here when you come back!' said Masher. When he had spoken, as if his anger had exhausted him or filled him with shame, a softer look entered Masher's face, his eyes reassumed their dark, heavy lustre once more, and he half-formed a smile in which there was something fatalistic and melancholy and then vanished into the room behind.

The boy left the shop with the sound of Mrs. Jonathan's voice complaining bitterly in his ears, and not daring to look back, hastened along the street, trembling a little and meeting the cold spring night with dry little gasps of his breath. The shoes, which he had not moved for a long time, seemed like stones on his back; and the string was cutting his shoulders like a wire and he dreaded that in time he would split apart, severed like a piece of cheese, and that the shoes and his body would fall into the dark abyss of the canal below.

By and by streets and houses of a different character

17

appeared; the windows of the houses were often brightly lighted, and the light would throw the shadows of carefully draped curtains and flowers and sometimes a bird in a cage on the yellow blinds. This was a world which Adam hardly knew, and into which, except when he went to Daniel's for Quintus or walked out with his grandmother, he did not often go.

Shops appeared, and these too were different; in these large, bright-windowed shops he felt it would be impossible to quarrel as he had just seen Masher quarrel with Mrs. Jonathan; and he felt that, like the houses, they were the embodiment of money, splendour, luxury and happiness, all the unattainable things he cherished in the depths of his mind.

We went on through streets brightly illuminated and crowded with traffic and people. The canal, the darkness, the mean streets were forgotten. Trams swung past him, swaying like boats and striking blue fire as they sailed away. A woman passed him carrying a basket of daffodils, and their heavenly fragrance, enveloping him like a light cloud, filled his heart with a sense of joy and a vague longing for something lovely, and the shoes seemed for a moment lighter.

Daniel's, the sewing-factory, lay beyond a dark archway at the foot of twenty or thirty steps, where some dark buildings were huddled confusedly in a yard. There was no one in the yard except a very old woman standing against a blank wall, spitting and coughing, the light from Daniel's window streaming faintly on her white hair.

The yard was filled with a drumming murmur of machines. As he pushed open the door of Daniel's, a low one-roomed building next to an empty house, this murmur suddenly leapt out at the boy like an infernal thing, shrieking and moaning and hammering as if his presence were hateful. He saw a confusion of fantastic machines

18

whirling and quivering and gleaming in gas light, worked by white-aproned men with faces shining with dirt and sweat; there were little smoking pots of wax hanging over fierce blue flames and hundreds of boots piled up about the machines. In that incessant activity no one paid any attention to him. There was a rank odour of burning wax and a machine which at intervals let out long shrieks more agonizing than all the rest shrieking together. He was frightened and in his fear he forgot the weight of the boots on his shoulder. He remained for some moments as if petrified, then a black individual, with eyes gleaming white and a dirty rag round his neck, seemed to bear down on him from nowhere, bellowed at him something startling and unintelligible, and snatched the boots from his shoulders before he could move or reply. The black individual vanished among the chaos of machines. Another machine began to shriek, and Adam felt that its voice increased a hundred-fold the infernal noise, the oppressive heat, the smell of burning wax and his own hatred of these things.

He waited for a long time, deafened and miserable. At last the black individual bore down on him again, the boots in his arms, and putting his mouth close to Adam's head, as though to bite off his ear, he shouted:

'Whose are they?'

'Quintus Harper's.'

'Harper's? Any money?'

'No.'

'Wait a minute.'

He vanished, and Adam hitched the boots to his shoulder and waited for him to return; he came at last with a folded piece of paper which he gave to Adam while shouting unintelligibly about Quintus.

When he had finished Adam stepped out into the yard. The world became marvellously still once more. The shrieking machines and the foul air of the sewing-factory were nothing; the old woman had disappeared, and he felt he was alone in a world of unbelievable calm shut in by the soft drapery of blue, untarnished sky.

As he walked slowly back through the lighted streets he saw signs of Easter everywhere, and he paused occasionally to look at the shops where eggs and yellow chickens were sold. There was also a flower-shop filled with narcissi and Lent lilies, and many blue and white and scarlet flowers whose names he did not know. The flowers made him remember that Christ was crucified, and that he was going to church with Quintus's daughter, Pauline, on Easter Sunday. It was Pauline who had taught him the difference between Lent lilies and daffodils.

When at last he reached Masher's again the oil was standing on a chair, and when he entered the shop Masher himself came through and told him to take it away.

There was still a smell of fish and Masher again had a book in his hand.

As Adam was leaving the shop with the oil Masher stopped him and said:

'Whose boy are you anyway? What's your name?'

'Adam Vance. Granny's name's Hosking.'

'Are the shoes heavy?'

'The string cuts my shoulders.'

'I'm coming up to Harper's, I'll carry them that little bit.'

He came out from behind the counter and lifted the shoes from Adam's shoulders and opened the door, and Adam stepped into the street with the oil. There was a hurried patter of feet and suddenly Mrs. Jonathan appeared and Masher paused on the doorstep.

'And so you're going out now?' she said in a derisive voice.

'I'm going out,' he said.

20

'Not content with standing up for that bloody twister, you must carry his shoes for him?'

'Yes, I'm carrying his shoes. They're heavy for the boy.'

'Yes? Wouldn't you like to carry the oil that he's had and'll never pay for?'

'Adam, give me the oil!' said Masher.

'Christ damn you! Damn you! Carrying the oil, you good Samaritan! Damn you!'

'Get along, Adam. I'm carrying the oil too. Get along!'

Masher stepped out into the street and closed the door and Mrs. Jonathan's abusive voice was cut off to a whisper. Masher and Adam went up Charlotte's Row in silence, walking slowly, and Adam was afraid either to look back or speak. As they passed the bakehouse he looked at the gas-jet still burning and saw the black shadow roaming over the ceiling as before. He caught the smell of baking bread and looked up into Masher's face with a remark on his lips about Good Friday, but he did not speak, for he felt he detected in Masher's face an expression of sad reflection and pain. And he felt suddenly that he liked Masher. He turned the echo of his words in his mind. He liked his pleasant, thoughtful face and the unusual air of restraint and assurance he bore even when taunted.

They turned down the dark side-passage of number seventeen. In the yard beyond this the darkness was broken up by a dirty orange light in the window of the shop where Quintus could be heard hammering the soles of shoes. The boy lifted the latch of the door and descended two steps into the shop. Quintus ceased hammering, squinted and pushed up his spectacles over his forehead into his hair.

'God Almighty, you've been a hell of a time,' he said.

'He had trouble,' said Masher, bringing in the boots and the oil.

'Trouble? Hello, Masher!'

21

Masher slung the boots over the bench and set the oil on the floor before speaking.

'He had trouble with the one who's plagued me for fifteen years too long.'

Quintus laid down his hammer, took out his snuff-box from a pocket under his apron, tapped it gently on his thumb and extended it without a word. The snuff-box was black and polished as ebony and was decorated with a nosegay of wild flowers on the lid in yellow, blue and rose. Masher and Quintus each took a pinch of snuff and sniffed it simultaneously. Quintus took a second pinch but Masher refused and Quintus blew his nose violently between his thumb and finger, sighing afterwards with pleasure.

Masher, with a motion of half-disgusted, half-weary resignation, closed the door slowly behind him, and the boy fell on his knees to warm his hands by the stove.

CHAPTER II

THE shop was low and small, like a cabin, and it reeked powerfully of dirt and leather. The white-washed walls were covered with innumerable wooden and iron lasts, hung in pairs; the floor was strewn with sacks and scraps of leather. A small oblong bench under the window was untidy with a litter of things: files, hammers, awls, soles, loose tacks, steel pins and rivets which danced and quivered whenever the shoemaker hammered. The lasts and the ceiling were draped with cobwebs that hung like mouse-coloured silken scarves. By the small stove, which the boy found with relief was alight, stood a sack of potatoes, and from the ceiling hung a rope of onions. There were curious odours besides the smell of leather, as if something had been left to rot in the dark corners.

A faint crimson glow was shining in the stove and for a long time the boy knelt before it, chafing back the blood into his white hands. Quintus filled a fresh lamp with oil and extinguished the first. The second lamp was painted scarlet except for a silvery reflector shaped like a scallop-shell, and Quintus hung it over the bench by the window.

The man called Masher approached the stove and sat by the side of the boy, on a chair with a splintered back. He also warmed his hands, chafing them slowly, and stared into the crimson light of the stove. His eyes still retained their expression of pensiveness mingled with the faintest melancholy. His face had a certain magnetic quality, a dreamy strength about it and a close, enigmatical air which attracted the boy. He sat as if lost in thought, and the boy studied him continuously.

Quintus pushed his spectacles over his nose and began hammering again. The work went on without interruption until a fresh voice suddenly remarked:

'Good evening, Masher.'

The boy, turning, saw in a corner behind him a small, insignificant creature dressed in a soft black hat and a shoddy black suit, as if in mourning. This was Quintus's brother Matthew. His voice was soft and ingratiating, his face white and meek, and the shining round orbs of his spectacles gave him alternately an air of sanctimonious aloofness and childlike stupidity.

'How d'you do?' said Masher curtly and fell silent at once again.

There was a note of cold dismissal in the words, a flash of weary scorn, and the man protested:

'Oh! be sociable, my friend. Try to speak in a spirit of brotherliness. What's biting you?'

'What's biting yourself?'

'Didn't you hear him,' broke in Quintus, 'say he'd had a bit of trouble? You keep your mouth shut! You talk like a bloody woman.'

'Quintus!'

'Tie your tongue in a knot for a minute, for God's sake!'

'Can't you remember, Quintus, that the boy is here?'

'What about the boy?'

'He hears everything.'

Quintus looked over his spectacles at the boy:

'Adam, my son,' he said, 'get yourself a tater and nozzle it down there in the warm ashes underneath the stove.'

He turned fiercely to his brother:

'He's got nobody, has he? Nobody only the old woman. Christ, he likes to come in here. You like to come and sit by the stove, don't you, eh, my son?'

'Yes.'

'I knew it. Put the tater under the stove, my son, and take no bloody notice of him, the daft blue-bottle.'

A never-resting feud existed between the brothers. Matthew, a Salvationist, talked systematically in terms of blood and forgiveness, consumed with an anxious desire to convert and reform. The shoemaker, who despised him for these things, was sick of his constant presence in the shop, and often threw him into the yard with voluble curses and blasphemous warnings never to return. Sooner or later, however, he would creep back again, sit idly in the shop hour after hour, and eventually resume entreating his brother to relinquish his evil ways. But Quintus was un-convertible and secretly Matthew was afraid of him, keep-ing carefully away whenever his drinking-fits came on. Quintus remained unchangeably idle, blasphemous, arro-gant, rebellious; he continued to drink like a beast, to love his dogs and spend his days dog-racing and ferreting. On the cold hillsides in the winter he was filled with the sharp primitive pride of hunting and the pleasure of breathing the wild air. Masher alone could reason with or influence him. The companionship of the two men was deep and curious. Quintus subjected himself to Masher, willingly assuming a second place, content merely to imitate and echo, crudely, blindly and often comically, his beliefs and philosophies. When Masher relinquished a worn-out creed and thrashed out for himself a new belief, Quintus listened, took it up also, tried to repeat it in the club and the bar, but always grew confused, his words clumsy and ineffectual beside the eloquence of Masher. Unable to talk with conviction, stammering with comical anger over such words as *millen-ium* and *proletariat*, he would drive home the argument with his fists, arguing the cause of the working-class in the very way Masher despised. Masher himself was a calm, reasoned speaker, passionate but unexcitable, disastrously

25

convincing. Very often he spoke with bitterness but more often with powerful simplicity and an underlying note of sadness in his voice, so that even the boy could understand, able to grasp unforgettably the injustice of the wretched houses in which he and the Harpers lived, the poverty, the filth, the miserable wages, the whole foul degradation of the existence they were condemned to endure. The boy, living with his grandmother on ten shillings a week and the little rent which the lodgers paid, understood the meaning of poverty and he felt vaguely that Masher stood for an existence in which poverty would find no place. He thought of this finer existence generally in terms of food, bitterly craving for something besides lard and dripping to eat with his bread. Under a changed condition of life, a life revolutionized, there would be pies, custard, chitterlings. Meanwhile he often turned over in his mind an expression of his grandmother's that seemed to him to represent that change beautifully and excitingly. Whenever he asked for some impossible luxury she would reply: 'You wait till the ship comes in,' and he believed that one day a ship with a white pyramid of sails all stiffly set in the sunshine would ride up the canal and come to rest below the railway-bridge. In this ship they would sail away.

As he sat by the stove he watched Masher intently, feeling that he stood for many of the things which he vaguely cherished in his own heart. And presently, impelled by his thoughts, he leaned forward and touching his sleeve, said timidly:

'Are you waiting for the ship to come in?'

Instantly, before Masher could turn or reply, Matthew sprang to his feet, held up his right hand with great dignity and half-chanted:

'Yes, my child, yes! He is waiting! He is waiting for the ship of the Lord God, the glorious ship that will take him and his sins away!'

Masher leapt to his feet also and retaliated:

'Sit down, you humbug!'

Matthew waved his arms and tried to utter a protest but his brother suddenly thundered:

'Make yourself small, blast you, you soft toad, d'ye hear? God Almighty!' he said slowly, with derision, 'if there wasn't something missing when you were put together! And d'ye hear me?' he shouted afresh. 'Any more of your soft humbug you go out of that door with a crack in the flapper you'll feel for a month, you bastard!'

Matthew opened his mouth to speak, but Quintus raised his hammer with a gesture of murderous ferocity, and Matthew sat down.

'And now,' said Quintus, turning to the boy, 'spit it out, young kipper.'

'Yes,' said Masher quietly, 'tell us what it is.'

The boy looked at Masher's dark eyes and prepared to speak, but the words had not begun to form themselves on his lips when the door opened. The two men turned at the sound of the latch and there appeared in the doorway the head and shoulders of a young girl of twenty. She was wearing a dress of dark green velvet with a collar of white lace; her face was pale and delicate, crowned by a mass of ebony black hair brushed smoothly back from her forehead and wound over her ears in the shape of two shallow black shells. She was tall and slender, with narrow shoulders and thin wrists, and her breast was swelling from girlhood to maturity. The expression of her face was dreamy and serious and while gazing from the door she brought her black eyebrows low over her bright eyes, as if in perplexity. To the boy she seemed very beautiful and he kept his eyes fixed unflinchingly upon her face, though she never looked at him.

'Come on to supper,' she said.

Her voice sounded low and even, and its tone was arresting. When she had spoken, her expression relaxed and her lips parted in a smile directed towards Masher. He also smiled and the smile of both of them was diffident and tender. In Masher's face there was also restraint; he appeared plainly half-afraid of smiling at her in the presence of others. With the girl it was different; her look was uncompromising and steady and in her dark eyes there was a look of undisguised pleasure and a hint of solemn adoration.

'I must go,' said Masher. The girl lowered her eyes.

Quintus stood pulling his apron over his head.

'Stay and have a glass of wine?' entreated the girl, raising her eyes a fraction. 'A little elderberry? Adam and I gathered the elderberries.'

'I ought to go,' said Masher.

'Good God, talk sense,' said Quintus. 'Here, Pauline, go and get another plate and another for your uncle. He'll come. And two extra glasses.'

'No, no, not for me,' protested Matthew. 'I've seen enough evil from the glass. Not for me.'

'God! dry up, blue-bottle! You don't drink, you don't bet, you don't swear. God knows what you find to do in life. Get the glasses, my gal!'

The girl vanished, and Masher, leaning against the door, stared into the darkness of the yard, as if gazing after her. Adam raked the potato from under the stove. The potato was blackened and hot and he rolled it to and fro in his hands. After Quintus had extinguished the lamp he climbed the two steps into the yard and stood for a moment in the darkness, gently tossing the potato from one hand to the other. There was a bright light in the Harper's window, the night air was still and frosty, and suddenly someone began to practise a song on a euphonium, picking out the tune laboriously and painfully. Quintus, Matthew and Masher followed him into the yard,

28

Quintus locked the shop and presently the three men went slowly into the house.

After the door had closed behind them the boy remained for some moments in the yard, listening to the tune from the euphonium. He knew that Quintus's eldest son George was playing. He was a tall thin fellow with a glass eye, and in the eyes of the boy he was a phenomenal figure. He often took out his glass eye and wiped it on his handkerchief as carelessly as a marble before slipping it back into its socket again. He played the euphonium badly, making it grunt like a sow. He looked very comical and faintly sinister, watching the music with one eye.

'How did you lose your eye?' the boy once asked.

'At school, an experiment.'

'What's an experiment?'

'Part of your education. Don't you know that! The teacher mixes things in a tube and heats the tube over a gas-burner. The tube exploded when I was holding it, that's all.'

'Why did it explode?'

'He was so damned ignorant he didn't know sulphur from sugar.'

The euphonium suddenly ceased and the night was silent. The boy left the Harpers' yard and went into the yard where he and his grandmother lived. The yard was dark except for a candle burning faintly in the kitchen window. When he opened the door he saw the candle, burning with a low splutter, standing on a bare deal table along with a loaf, a basin of yellow dripping, a salt-pot and a basin painted prettily at the rim with scarlet flowers and emerald leaves. At the table, her grey hair and the wrinkled skin of her half-shrewd, half-kindly face yellowish in the feeble light, his grandmother was sitting, a woman between sixty and seventy, rapidly knitting with black needles and coarse grey wool, her head bent very low over her needles towards the candle-flame. She was wearing a tight-necked dress of black material worn to glossiness, and there were scores of miniature jet beads on her bosom that glittered and trembled as she moved the needles. She put down her knitting, greeted him and rose immediately in order to cut him a slice of bread.

'Quintus gave me a tater,' said Adam, 'with pink spots on.'

'That's all right. That's a King Edward,' she said. 'You're late coming in.'

She spoke quickly but softly, and in her movements she was quick and darting, like a bird. Adam sat down and pulled off his shoes.

'I went to Daniel's for Quintus and then I roasted the tater. Do I want bread with a tater?'

'Yes. You can have a bit of bread. You want salt too,' she said.

She broke open the potato for him and sprinkled salt on the steaming halves. The boy took the bread in one hand and some potato in the other and sat at the table. Before eating he pondered over the potato; it seemed to him suddenly like an egg and he was reminded again of Easter. The woman picked up the basin and began slowly sucking something from a spoon.

'What's that?' he asked, swallowing potato.

'A bit of arrowroot,' she said.

He looked at her steadfastly.

Suddenly she held out a spoonful of arrowroot and he leaned forward and licked the spoon. She smiled faintly and asked if it were good, and he nodded, his tongue too occupied to speak.

After he had finished the potato and she had eaten the arrowroot she made him take off his collar and wash at the small yellow sink in the corner. While drying his face he gazed round the room; it was very small and the walls were hung with paper varnished a dirty-shining brown. Here and there the paper had worn completely away or was hanging loose from the wall in drooping shreds, showing naked patches of plaster. There was no furniture except the deal table, an old sewing machine covered with a black cloth, some chairs and a set of shelves painted a dull vermilion and stocked with medicine bottles and a book or two. The fire in the grate was low and dismal and the air was strong with an unpleasant acrid smell of burning leather.

'I went to Jonathan's,' said the boy, 'for some oil. Mrs. Jonathan wouldn't let me have it until Masher came in. And then they quarrelled and she threw something at him. He carried the oil for me when I came back.'

'When you've finished washing I want you to come here,' she said.

'They hate each other I think,' said the boy. 'She threw some fish at him and gobbed in his face.'

'Ah! be quiet! That's not our business. If you've finished come here!' she said sharply.

Presently the boy hung the towel over the sink again and went slowly towards her.

'Kneel down,' she said, and he knelt before her, his head resting in her lap in an attitude of prayer.

She moved the candle across the table so that the light fell on his head, making his hair shine like pale yellow silk in the rays. She herself was sitting so that her shadow fell away from him. 'Whenever you go down to Daniel's,' she said in a faintly vexed tone, 'I get an idea you're lousy.' She began to run her hands with a rapid motion over his scalp, conducting a minute investigation, pressing his hair apart inch by inch with her rough fingers. Whenever, hating the prickling pain at the roots of his hair and the sensation of being imprisoned by her, he squirmed and tried to release himself, she reprimanded him sharply and

31

her fingers seemed to search even more harshly and inexorably. 'You don't want your head to be alive, do you?' she said. 'I should think not.' Suddenly he would feel the crack of her fingers on his skull, a low 'Ach!' of disgust from her and a fresh injunction to keep his head within the circle of candlelight.

Presently the crack would be repeated and he would ask: 'What was that?' and she would reply in a tone of disgust, never lessening her hold upon his head, 'Nits! You'd have been lousy in the morning. Hold still. My mother had sixteen of us and we were never lousy and I'll see you ain't either.' She explored every inch of his hair from his soft forelock down to the nape of his neck until his spine ached and he bitterly hated the scrupulous searching of her fingers. When the search and the sharp click of her fingers had ceased at last she bade him stand up and she then proceeded to comb his hair over the sink, holding the candle above his head with one hand and the sharp tooth-comb in the other. He hated this also; the comb dragged fiercely and painfully at the tangles her hands had made.

When at last she released him she gave him a second stump of candle in an old brass holder and kissed him. He took the candle with relief and began to ascend the stairs, half-troubled, half-fascinated by the enormity of his shadow creeping beside him like a black monster on the dirty wall. He heard her last warning injunction as he set foot on the stairs, a whispered, 'Be quiet, remember!' which left the house hushed, a little terrifying to him in its hollow silence. In the two other rooms of the house the lodgers lived, a young workman and his wife and child. He knew he must be silent because of the baby. Occasionally he would go in to see the lodgers; the husband was thin and dark, with bright carmine spots on his cheeks, and the wife seemed no more than a girl. He had once or twice seen the girl sitting before the fire with the baby at her breast, trying to suckle it. Her tender white breasts were no larger than blown roses, and the baby seemed to obtain no satisfaction from them, fretting constantly. To him they seemed a simple, timid pair, bound up in each other and desperately fond of the thin white child. In the dead of night he often heard the baby crying and in the daytime the mother could be heard prattling and laughing with it, her voice tremulous with ripples of devoted joy.

Because of the lodgers he slept in the same room as his grandmother, in a huge iron skeleton of a bed pushed against the wall. He set the candle on a chest of drawers and undressed himself, blew out the candle and lay down against the wall.

Before falling asleep he again remembered that it would soon be Easter and he reminded himself of the note from Daniel's, which he had forgotten to give to Quintus. Lying in the dim state between wakefulness and sleep he fancied once or twice that he heard voices in the yard outside. The night was clear and still and he told himself that he could hear the voices of Pauline and Masher talking in the yard, but raising himself on his elbow and straining in order to listen better he could hear nothing, and the night relapsed into stillness again except for a night-train rushing over the bridge with echoing thunder.

CHAPTER III

ON Easter Sunday morning nine white pigeons were circling swiftly in the blue air over the backyards of Charlotte's Row, their wings making a sighing sound which rose and fell to a whisper as they surged overhead and wheeled away.

The pigeons belonged to a house-painter named Pinkney, a short, comical-looking man with rolling black eyes and a stiff black growth of beard, who spoke with a lisp. He was leaning against a water-barrel, smoking the end of a cigarette and gazing up at his birds with languid pleasure. The shadows of the pigeons travelled swiftly over the grey roofs, the grey oblong yards adjoining the houses and the narrow strips of black earth beyond. The gardens were unkept and bare except for some occasional half-frozen stalks of cabbage leaves. Under the long wall enclosing the gardens the painter had built a pigeon-house, and adjoining it the Harpers kept their ferrets in a little wooden hutch white-washed inside and out. There were often quarrels over the ferrets and the pigeons.

'Curth your blathted animalth, Quintuth,' the painter would storm.

'What's wrong with 'em, eh?'

'They'll thcare the bloody life out of my birdth!'

'And a damn good job! We'll have pigeon-pie then and something good for once!'

'Thath all very well. But what do you think I am? One of the blathted arithtocrathy? Pigeonth cotht money.'

'You're one of the great army of the proletariat, that's all you are. A bloody flea.'

34

'Whoth a flea?'

'You're a flea. We're all fleas. But them ferrets are my ferrets and where they stand is my garden and whether you blasted well like it or not they'll stand there as long as I can take a pinch of snuff! And don't forget it!'

Sometimes the argument would grow more heated and the women would join in; and once Quintus had flown into a rage and had rushed backwards and forwards with innumerable buckets of water, throwing them with tempestuous curses at the painter's kitchen door.

Quintus was not to be seen on Easter Sunday morning. On Sundays he did not stir before midday, and then came down in a bad temper, too sick to eat, and pressed a cold cup to his head with groaning sighs before going out to his club, from which he returned at two o'clock, to sleep again. Only Adam and the painter were in the yard. The boy was standing in his grandmother's patch of garden, blinking his eyes as he gazed at the pigeons wheeling gracefully in the sunshine.

When the pigeons had circled round a great many times the Harpers' door opened and Pauline came into the yard. She was carrying a blue enamel bowl and had nothing on over her white underskirt. A black water-barrel stood by the house and she came and leaned over the barrel and dipped her bowl into the water. She saw the pigeons and she stood with the full bowl of water resting just beneath her breast and looked up at them. The bare flesh of her neck and shoulders was very sallow and the sunlight falling full on her face and into her eyes gave her a look of freshness that made her seem very young.

Adam called her by name and slowly came from the garden towards her.

'I'm all ready,' he said to her.

He stood still.

'Not for church?' she exclaimed.

'Yes.'

She leaned back a little over the barrel, curving out her white bosom, and looked at him. The boy was wearing an ill-fitting jacket of coarse grey cloth and a pair of snuff-coloured corduroys reaching below his knees, a pair of thick heavy black boots and a broad celluloid collar tied with a thin black bow. The coat and the boots he was wearing for the first time; they were secondhand, but not much worn, and he was wearing them with boyish pride and satisfaction. They had been bought for him from a secondhand clothes-dealer, who sold everything from the cast-off gowns of ladies to the uniform of a hussar.

He stood almost to attention, awkward and expectant as the girl looked at him.

'Will I do?' he said.

'Will he do, Mr. Pinkney, do you think?' she said to the painter.

The painter, looking up, held his cigarette between his thumb and forefinger, puffed out a cloud of smoke and spat. 'Leth have a look at you,' he said. The boy stood even more stiffly and awkwardly and the painter eyed him slowly up and down with his large eyes. After a minute he spoke.

'Well God bleth your belly!' he exclaimed suddenly. 'Who put your shoeth on?'

'Granny.'

'Well jutht look at them!'

Adam and Pauline gazed at the boy's feet, saw nothing wrong and glanced up again, mystified.

'What's wrong with the shoes?'

'Well jutht look at them!'

He burst into a loud cackle, like an overjoyed hen.

'What is it?' they asked.

The girl was impatient and the boy felt uneasy and pained.

36

'Well, God thave the King!' He doubled himself against the water-butt and cackled again.

'But what is it?'

'Go in!' he urged them. 'Go in and let your mother thee before I have a blethed fit!'

He waved them into the house, cackling and spitting with laughter.

Slowly, very mystified and hurt, the boy followed Pauline into the house. Now and then the girl looked back at him, puzzled also, spilling water from the bowl as she turned.

'Mother, come here, what's wrong with Adam's shoes?'

They entered a little kitchen, painted an ugly green colour and overcrowded with furniture, and a little woman with a fat pink cherubic face and little blue humorous eyes came in answer to Pauline's question. She gazed steadily at Adam's big ugly boots while the girl looked on.

'God love us!' she suddenly exclaimed.

'What is it?'

'God love us! But look at them! They're left to right!'

She laughed uproariously. The boy was made to sit in a chair while Pauline took off the left boot and her mother the right. Adam sat for a moment without his shoes. The shoes were heavy and his toes were crumpled and it was very comfortable without them.

'Can I sit in my stockings a minute?' he begged.

'God love the boy, sit in them till Pauline washes herself. Are you hungry?'

'I had my breakfast.'

'There's a hot-cross bun left. Could you find room for that?'

He stared, murmured a faint 'Yes' and Mrs. Harper brought him the bun.

'Thank you.' He looked at the bun and turned it over. 'It ain't got a cross on,' he observed.

'It's one of old Come-to-Jesus's,' she said. 'He don't put crosses on. He thinks he'd go to hell if he did. He don't put currants neither. Still it's a bun. And that's everything.'

'I wish it'd got a cross on.'

'Ah! the cross don't make no difference. Get it down you.'

Adam began to eat the bun and Pauline began to wash her face and hands at the sink in the corner. The boy watched her. The kitchen, smelling rankly of stale cooking, was dirty and sordid, and nothing attracted the boy except a black oak box standing in one corner, half-covered with an emerald-green cloth blazing with a golden harp. He longed to know what was in the box and why the cloth was there. His gaze stole towards the corner and rested upon it, while he ate the bun absently, trying to fathom the mystery.

While he was thus occupied the girl slipped down her bodice and washed her chest and began to hum in a soft voice. She was conscious of being very happy, and she lost herself for a moment in pondering joyously over the fragment of blue sky visible from the window. She was humming an Easter hymn set to an old German tune and as she dried her face and breast a faint pink flush stole over her skin, giving her a strange radiance.

In the other room her one-eyed brother was sitting at a table, drinking a cup of tea and reading a Sunday newspaper. In his shirt-sleeves he looked indolent, sleepy and rather sinister. Two other brothers, wearing white neckerchiefs and holding the two fawn-coloured harriers on the leash, came in at the back-door and said something to the one-eyed one. All three went outside, and in a few moments Pauline's only sister, Fanny, a heavy, pasty-faced woman far gone in pregnancy, came downstairs and sat in her brother's place. Her husband had been killed in an explosion. There had been difficulties over compensation. Her face was sombre, tragic, brooding. No one wanted the baby, and occasionally the widow had fits of despondency when she declared with bitter vehemence that she would have been glad to die. She sat staring into the fire and did not move when Mrs. Harper appeared with an ironing-board and balanced it between a table and a chair and began ironing a scarlet dancing-dress.

The dress was astonishingly beautiful, low at the bodice and with fine red skirts lying countlessly one beneath another. On the far side of the town Mrs. Harper's sister let out apartments and occasionally among her lodgers there was a variety actress. On such occasions Mrs. Harper would be sent lovely amazing dresses to wash. Pauline left the kitchen in order to look at the dress and held a corner of it against the faintly flushed nakedness of her bosom so that the scarlet seemed to blaze against her pallor.

'Why can't I have a dress like that?' she said.

'What else?' Mrs. Harper smacked the iron down on the dress.

Pauline stood at the door. 'I should have a dress like that if things were equal,' she said.

'Things ain't equal. They never will be.'

Suddenly the girl's eyes flashed and a note of half-angry insistence entered her voice:

'But they will be! People won't lie for ever to be trampled in the muck. There'll be a turn of the wheel and then things will be different. It might come to-morrow and it might come in twenty years, but it'll come, and then this rotten state of things will be crushed and forgotten, thank God!'

She spoke with passionate insistence, but also half as if she were repeating some formula she had heard persistently. There was something about her words that was vague and idealistic, as if she were not certain as to how or when this change in life would come, but was only anxious for its coming because it seemed to her beautiful and just.

She left the room and could be heard going upstairs. The elder sister had not moved; Mrs. Harper drew the red dress over the ironing-board and Adam began to put on his shoes. Finally he went into the living-room. He had tied the laces in knots and the loose ends were flapping about his shoes.

He stood watching the red frills of the dress being turned on the ironing-board.

Presently Pauline came down, dressed in a carefully kept grey costume and carrying a pair of pale grey gloves in her hand. As if angry she passed through the room without speaking and Adam followed her into the yard.

In the yard the painter was busy housing his pigeons and a group of women, some nursing babies, stood watching him. Pauline walked hastily along by the mean houses, along the passage and into the street. Depressed by the pitiful sordidness revealed in the sunshine and by her mother's indifference, it seemed to her ironical that the street outside should be cold and plunged in shadow and that Adam should delay behind her. She called impatiently and he caught her up, wondering and looking up, and for a long time he half-ran, half-walked at her side, while she said nothing. Beyond the railway-bridge the sunshine was warm again and the canal lay still, like a sheet of silver; the factories were silent and the deserted streets were strange and peaceful. Troubled by the words that had leapt spontaneously from her lips, the girl found herself going back to the occasion when she had heard them spoken, and in the spring sunshine the revolution, the miracle, the change in life, seemed to her alive with fresh importance and beauty.

They crossed the tram-lines and passed rows of shops and the steps leading to Daniel's sewing-factory and entered a maze of streets beyond. No trams were running; pieces of dirty paper were blowing forlornly along the shining tram-lines. At one place a person had been sick and there was a pool of darkened blood and then for some distance there ran a trail of brighter blood, like a line of crimson coins, running on and on. In the neighbourhood a bell began to ring and somewhere a brass-band began to play *Christ our Lord is Risen* and the music and the bells quarrelled and jangled one against another. Presently another and another bell began to ring, until the whole peal of bells was clanging, half-jubilantly, half-chaotically. A fat woman hurried past, breathing through her coarse red lips, like a fish; on her bosom she was wearing a bunch of violets and the air was beautiful with their fragrance long after she had gone.

The thoughts in the girl's mind continued to be half-joyous, half-troublesome. Occasionally she looked behind her, as if expecting to see someone coming. In her sudden spasms of happiness there was a tremor of sadness which slowly mastered her but in which before long she found a new, incongruous, comforting sense of joy.

She would see a group of men talking at a street corner and stop abruptly; the boy would stop too. Without warning she would look confused and with the same faint flush in her pallor would begin to walk on again.

'What did you stop for?' he would say.

'I don't know.'

'What did you want?' he would insist.

'I don't know. I thought I'd forgotten something.'

They came to within sight of the church; the spire pointing upward among the dirty roofs looked fresh and golden in the sunlight; an almond-tree was blooming in the churchyard, pink and graceful, like a cloud. Among the

41

mounds there were gay rings of daffodils nodding and bow-ing like groups of old-fashioned dancers.

The bells were still ringing loudly and people were hurrying in under the porch. Going in, Pauline and Adam sat behind a white pillar, the girl intent and dreamy, the boy with his gaze fixed upon the altar decorated with Lent lilies and daffodils and nosegays of pale wild wind-flowers that were already drooping and forlorn. The church was very beautiful and the air was coloured with faint rain-bows where the sun came down from the stained windows. There was a fragrance of something beautifully old mingled with the odour of candles and the scent of daffodils.

The service began. When the prayers came the girl knelt with her head pressed against her hands and prayed passionately and ardently for the fulfilment of vague desires; she prayed without listening to the prayers of the service and the words came pouring torrentially through the darkness of her mind, sweeping away doubt and sad-ness; in the clearness of her mind after her words had exhausted themselves she became suddenly conscious of the face of Masher and his dark, enigmatical, profound eyes fixed upon her; in the darkness she returned his look with a soft, uncompromising gaze and slowly her heart filled with ecstasy of pleasure that left her trembling.

Raising his head cautiously from between his fingers, Adam looked at her and saw her hands clenched, her whole being intent and her face radiant with a rapture he did not understand.

When the service was over the girl came into the sun-shine with a feeling of vague elation. She was not yet cer-tain what she felt towards Masher. She was conscious only of a certain pleasure in his presence, in listening to his conversation, in evoking for herself his words and his appearance when he was no longer with her. She was fond

42

of the service in the same vague way and for the same uncertain motives. There was something inexplicably comforting in the thought of prayer and something aesthetic in the quiet solemnity of the church itself that touched her sense of beauty. She would accept the words of the service readily, not questioning or denying their truth, carried away by their solemnity and her belief in God. She herself knew only that she believed in God and she hardly ever questioned herself. Her mind was like a young plant, shaken by whatever wind blew, as ready to be inspired by the words of the Church as the ideals of Masher, simple, virgin, half-awake, like the mind of a child. Her beliefs and desires were passionate and uncompromising. She was ready to fall at the feet of Christ and worship ecstatically and with her whole being, without asking or needing a reason. She was as ready to devote herself to Masher; there was something profoundly inspiring in his ideals and something to excite her youthful passion and her need for beauty in his enigmatical eyes, his soft voice, his indefinable masculinity. And in whatever she chose to do she felt that she would never relax or falter in her devoted intensity; she would never waver or look back.

The streets which had been deserted in the early morning were crowded with church-goers and loafers standing at corners or walking aimlessly up and down. The girl often looked among the faces in the hope of seeing Masher. Mountains of white clouds were beginning to sail solemnly across the blue sky, their shadows chasing each other up the narrow streets through which Adam and Pauline were passing.

They took a shorter way home and passed the factory where the girl worked. The place was old, ill-planned and dirty; the walls rose up dark and gaunt, forming an ugly block in which windows of thick glass were placed at intervals; the windows were foul with oil and dust and there was a stench of machinery and leather. There was an impression of confinement and darkness. The girl worked in the topmost story, alternately skiving pieces of leather or treadling a sewing machine. The room was narrow and low and not large enough to accommodate the thirty women and girls who worked at the machines and benches, sitting on round wooden stools set too closely together. The sound of the sewing-machines was furious and incessant and from below a constant throbbing of heavier machinery shook the floor and sounded like distant thunder. In summer the sun burned fiercely down on the unlathed roof until the room was stifling with the sweltering heat of an oven. During the winter it seemed as if the frost sometimes froze even the treadles of the machines, so that the girl often sat in the darkness of a winter morning with hatred and bitter misery in her heart, her fingers too dead to feel the cotton, her feet, frozen and bloodless, working mechanically as if no longer part of her.

When they reached home the house-painter was cutting the hair of a half-bald little fat man sitting outside in the sunshine, with a woman's apron tucked round his neck. The boy stayed to watch, fascinated by the painter steering the scissors among the heavy fat of the man's neck without cutting him.

'Well, Adam!'

The painter gave his scissors a fantastic flourish over his head and spat into the yard.

'You thee,' he said. 'I can do other thingth bethideth paint. I can hair-dreth, I can mend watcheth and I'm a bit of a carpenter. Now let me give you a pieth of advithe. Never have jutht one trade. You thee? Eh? Alwayth plenty of tradeth!' He gave a triumphant flourish with the scissors. 'Mark my wordth! Alwayth plenty of tradeth!'

44

'And you mark my bloody neckhole!' said the customer angrily.

'Thath all right! Don't worry!'

'I ain't worrying! But I don't want to be stuck like a pig, do I, fathead? Here, you run along, my son,' he said to Adam. 'He'll stick my gizzard or some fine thing, talking to you.'

Obediently the boy walked slowly away, into the Harper's kitchen. He was to eat his dinner there, as he often did on Sundays. The warm smell of the food already cooking came sweetly to him, awaking his hunger sharply.

At half-past twelve he sat down with the family. The Harpers took their meals without ceremony. The sons began to eat immediately the food was passed along the table to them, ravenous as dogs, their heads brooding over their plates, their arms sprawling over the dirty table-cloth; the food was never chewed, but drawn in between their lips with loud sucking noises, revolved hastily on their tongues and bolted; they periodically spat out scraps of gristle and fat which the two harriers, waiting devotedly behind the chairs, also bolted; they ate as if racing each other, rarely speaking or looking up, pausing only to belch or feed the dogs. Their plates were very often scraped white again before Mrs. Harper and the daughters had begun.

Adam sat between Pauline and her mother. Mrs. Harper was at the head of the table, Adam on her left hand and the widowed sister Fanny on her right. The widow stared at her food vacantly, as if sick; presently she tasted something half-heartedly, but immediately began to stare again and finally dropped her knife and fork and gave it up. The brother with one eye said something to her; she shook her head and he reached over and took her share, leaving her staring at the place where the plate had been. It was oppressively warm in the room and there was a powerful

45

odour of vinegar. The sons took vinegar with most of their food, even fresh meat and vegetables. To-day they ate for a long time, demanding fresh helpings, drenching each plateful heavily with vinegar. Having finished they leaned back in their chairs, rocked themselves to and fro, belched with satisfaction and picked their teeth with spent match-stalks. Quintus was not there; he had risen late and had vanished immediately with a black scarf round his neck, his face very yellow and dissipated.

Mrs. Harper was keeping a plate of food for him in the oven. Presently the sons pushed back their chairs and called the harriers into the yard and the women and Adam were left to finish eating alone.

They sat for a short time without speaking; then Pauline rose and began to make some tea, Adam clinking the spoons into the saucers for her. It was pleasant and restful without the men and the tea was sipped slowly and dreamily, as if to prolong this pleasure. The voices of the men calling the dogs seemed far away. Pauline and Adam gazed into the fire, sitting side by side on the hearth-rug; Mrs. Harper and Fanny leaned their arms on the table, looking over the coloured pictures of an old fashion maga-zine.

A sudden scuffle in the yard made Mrs. Harper leap up, hasten to the window and peer out. Outside there were thick, argumentative voices.

'God love us!' she said. She flew back to the oven. 'He's coming already.'

'Who is it?' said Pauline half-rising.

'Your father. You best get up and sit on the couch until he's done.'

'Bring your tea on the couch, Adam, and sit by me.'

Adam followed the girl to the dilapidated black couch and they sat down, holding the cups on their knees. There was a sudden scraping of heavy boots at the door and a loud voice demanding several times: 'Where's the dinner, eh? Where's the dinner?'

Everyone was silent; the door opened noisily and Quintus came in. He was faintly flushed, his eyes were excited and watery, he swaggered. Behind him, overshadowed by his great bulk, came a little shoddy man, with shifty red eyes and a look of perpetual cringing and fear on his face; his face was dry, lean and colourless and was half-swallowed by a grotesque greenish-black bowler coming down low over his ears and forehead; his ill-fitting clothes had turned green with time and he was smoking a cigarette which caused him to cough perpetually and spit at intervals as if violently asthmatical. He looked ill at ease. Quintus was dragging him by the sleeve and apparently he resented this, for he suddenly released himself, thrust his hands gloomily into his pockets and hung backward.

Quintus swaggered up to the table and again demanded the dinner in a loud voice, staring at everyone with lugubrious hostile eyes. Mrs. Harper stood and regarded him stolidly.

'The dinner's ready when you are,' she said.

'Well, look slippy, woman, let's have it!'

'Who do you think you're ordering?' Her eyes were burning with contempt and she was drawn up to him.

'Christ! who am I ordering? You'd lip me would you?'

'Yes, I'd lip you,' she said.

'Well, lip me again and I'd squash your bloody face to jelly! See? Christ help us! Sit down, Slommax, take your hat off. I'll hope there'll be a mouthful for me friend Slommax?' he said.

'Your own dinner's in the oven, waiting,' she said.

'Me own dinner? What the hell d'ye mean by that? Sit down, Slommax.'

Slommax was afraid to sit down.

47

'Sit down, Slommax!'

'I'd best be going,' said the little man.

'Sit down I tell you!' he roared. The man came slowly forward and sat on the edge of a chair, in extreme consternation. His little red eyes were blinking rapidly.

'And now let's have a bite, damn you! Get it out! Can't you see there's a visitor, eh? Can't you see me friend Slommax is here, eh?'

'Your own dinner's in the oven, waiting,' she said.

He suddenly lurched forward and thrust his black, excited face into hers, showing his teeth and curving his mouth in contempt, and she seemed by contrast ludicrously small and defenceless, her face very like a shining red apple, her eyes blue and unflinching as she returned his hostile glare.

'Blast you! Put the food on the table, then!' he shouted. 'That's what you're here for, ain't it?' Suddenly he stopped and saw the cups. 'Oh! I see,' he said softly, mocking, 'they're drinking tea. I didn't know that. My mistake. Of course. Tea. The wife sits drinking her tea, Slommax, while the bread-winner dies of starvation! Go on, drink your tea, drink your blasted tea! Slommax and me can starve.'

'Starve! you've enough beer in your bellies to keep you alive for a week!'

'Eh, what's that?' he said quickly.

'You heard what I said, Quintus Harper, you heard well enough what I said.'

'Say it again!'

'I wouldn't waste my breath.'

'Say it again, I say! Christ! I'd like to hear you say it again!'

She turned away with a sudden motion of indifferent contempt. An iron spoon lay on the table and she picked it up and played with it for a moment with the same contemptuous air, ignoring him. All the pride in his nature was suddenly incensed by this and with his eyes flaming he sprang forward, snatched the spoon from her and flung it into her face. The handle of the spoon struck her mouth and the spoon rolled away with dull rings beneath the sofa. Blood crimsoned her mouth and a startled expression like that of a frightened animal's came into her wide eyes.

For a moment she stood perfectly still. Her mouth was pursed very tightly. The blood began to run in a spidery rivulet from her thin lips. The fear in her eyes gave way to her previous contempt, and she turned suddenly away from him with her former cold indifference.

He was sullenly alarmed at the sight of blood. 'Did I catch you?' he said, half-following her.

She flung up her head but did not move her lips. Pauline sprang to her feet and said something which Harper did not catch and they exchanged glances. The inference in the girl's look incensed him afresh.

'And what are you up on your hind-legs for, my lady?' he roared.

'Don't speak to him,' said her mother. 'Sit down, my darling, where you were and don't speak to him.'

'Speak to me! Christ! My own daughter'll speak to me when she's spoken to, I warrant! What is it, my lady?'

'You're too drunk to be spoken to.'

'What's that?'

'I say you're drunk and the other one's drunk too. But thank God he slipped off while his shoes were good. There's too many mouths to feed in this house already, without that miserable toad.'

Harper swung round. He roared when he saw the empty chair where his friend had been sitting. He rushed to the door, lurching against the furniture, and bellowed for Slommax.

In a moment he came back, stood slightly swaying and

49

glanced with quivering red eyes first at Pauline and then at her mother.

'Jesus wept,' he muttered bitterly. 'I bring me friends home to dinner and my wife and daughter turn them out again. Hospitality! Very nice. Oh yes, very nice! Damn you!'

'That's enough,' said Pauline. 'For God's sake that's enough.'

'What's that you're saying?'

'Eat your dinner.'

'Shut your mouth, my lady!' he roared.

'Perhaps you'll shut it for me?'

'Nice daughters I've got! Nice wife and nice daughters!'

The widowed daughter suddenly lifted her apron and began to cry.

'Don't cry, don't mind him.' Pauline stared at him. 'He's too drunk to know what he's saying.'

'That's a lie! Get out of this house, with your blasted lies! Get out!'

He thrust his head slightly forward, ponderously, menacing her. She suddenly turned and bent to the oven and picked up the plate of meat and potatoes and slapped it on the table before him. He watched her with infuriated eyes.

'That's what you've whined and carried on for, isn't it? Now eat it.'

'Hold your tongue! Get out! Didn't I tell you to get out!'

'That's all right. I'm going.'

'Then get out before I kick you out!'

She suddenly turned, found her hat and jacket and walked out of the house.

'You damn stuck-up bitch!' he shouted after her.

The mother stood with one hand resting upon the table;

50

with the other she was dabbing her lips. Fanny sat silent, the tears drying on her white cheeks, her expression vacant. With a sullen gesture Quintus sat down and began to eat, swilling his food with vinegar. The bitter, sour smell of the vinegar floated slowly through the room. The shoemaker ate like his sons, ravenously, his head low down, his eyes fixed moodily on his plate, his expression threatening and churlish. Occasionally he muttered complainingly to himself, as if to indicate that he had been very much wronged. Presently, with a fierce gesture of his hand he suddenly muttered, 'Bah!' and pushed the food away in disgust. The plate overbalanced and the meat and vegetables spilled on the tablecloth, the vinegar running rapidly away in a brown stain.

'Think I can eat that muck?' he yelled. 'Bah!'

He staggered away from the table, wrenched open the door and stumbled upstairs. The women heard the heavy thuds of his feet above and the mighty creak of the bed-springs as he flung himself down. The widow burst into tears again and her mother, staring at the faintly reeking food, exclaimed fiercely:

'God! If you were to die this minute, you devil, I'd dance on the ceiling!'

She raised her face and shook her fist at him. Simultaneously there were two powerful thuds in the room above. She sat down again. She knew that Quintus had thrown his boots at the bed-room wall.

CHAPTER IV

A NORTH-BOUND boat train passed over the bridge at
Charlotte's Row shortly before eight o'clock on Sunday
evenings. The line skirted the town, running side by side
with the canal for a mile or more, so that the passengers
looking out on one side would see nothing but tall factories and warehouses casting sombre, perpendicular
shadows into the water and nothing on the other but endless grey rows of concrete houses, bordered by narrow
gardens turned black with smoke. As the factories ceased
and the houses became fewer and the line turned away
from the canal, steering straight into open country, the
land spread out flat and treeless except for solitary ashes
and occasional twisted hawthorn-trees. The canal itself
flowed onward in a rigid, unwavering line like a steel ruler,
its low bank barren of trees also. Just beyond the outskirts
of the town a brickyard, a cluster of five slender red chimneys surrounded at their feet by squat black kilns, stood
on the edge of a clay-pit. The banks of the pit were steep,
coloured a dark blue like thunder-clouds, and the water
lying still and dark between, of great depth, was thickly
fringed with withered sedge and tall spears of yellow
reeds.

Masher Jonathan had worked at the brick-yard for
twenty years. Adjoining the yard was a field which the
men shared in plots, cultivating flowers and vegetables
and an occasional fruit-tree. Masher had begun at the
brick-yard as a boy; from the very first he had disliked the
work consistently, always hoping for something better
without having the courage necessary to break away and

change. As a boy he hated to lose his freedom and sacrifice himself to the tall chimneys he could see against the sky as soon as he woke in the morning and the kilns whose hot breath scorched him and dried his veins. The lean, dry, knotty character of his face had been shaped by the work. His body, small-boned, lithe, compact, had never been the body of a typical worker. His hands were small, and the fingers though thick and muscular from labour, were sensitive and light as a woman's fingers. He walked airily, in a quick, lilting fashion. He could carry a bunch of flowers, even a spray of lilies, with a natural grace and without a sense of awkwardness. He had a passionate love of the countryside, a longing to be part of it, as it were to satisfy some primeval desire to be part of earth again; his feeling for flowers was exquisite, tender, unusual. The two powerful feelings were constantly wrenching at him. His longing to give way to them was almost a melancholy thing, like a desire that can never be satisfied. At intervals he wanted to break away from the brickyard and the filthy poverty of the town and tramp off somewhere, seeking a fresh life, but he was bound by a feeling for humanity, a capacity for pitying his fellow-men that weighed on him like an obligation. All his socialism and schemes for the betterment of mankind were full of something sadly impractical and a little disillusioned, as if at the bottom of his heart he were half-convinced, and faintly afraid, that they could come to nothing. In the plot of land that he cultivated in the shelter of a hawthorn hedge by the brickyard he found something to console him; he could put into this piece of earth his love of beauty, all his instinct for creation, and imagine vaguely that he saw in the faces of flowers the fulfilment of his desires.

He had worked under the shelter of the hawthorn hedge throughout Easter Sunday, setting the first potatoes. Towards eight, soon after the express had passed northward, Pauline came slowly down the canal path. She walked aimlessly. The sun had gone down and a stronger breeze was beginning to flutter the soft green shoots of hawthorn and the bush of sloe-blossom, white as frozen snow, waving gracefully beyond the black wooden hut on Masher's plot.

That afternoon the girl, miserably angry after the scene with Quintus, had gone off into the country. Beyond the town on the southward side the countryside became beautiful in a peaceful, unassuming way, the land spreading out into long vistas of soft low hills set with plantations of fir and pine; in the hollows rested villages and farms half-obscured by sapling-copses; between the woodlands lay long sheltered sweeps of pasture as green and smooth as the lawns of great houses. The big industrial town in its squalid hollow was hidden and forgotten. As the girl left the town and ascended gently to the higher land and saw the fresh country unfolding itself, the soft switch-back of green hills undulating into a distance of cloudy blue, she experienced a feeling of wildest joy. The sun was still shining, tenderly warm, like a child's breath. The white clouds sailing aloft looked cold, like snow. There were signs of spring, pillows of sloe-blossom on the black hedges, a sycamore bursting to sharp green over the pond in a farm-yard, a man in yellow corduroys moving about among a restless, pretty company of white lambs. She gazed at all this with a dazed, almost stupid pleasure, as though her mind were still dulled by the long winter and the town.

As she went on, walking throughout the whole afternoon from village to village, this dazed pleasure and the feeling of wild joy gave way to a sensation of continuous, smoothly flowing, happiness. Her anger at Quintus's drunkenness abated; the disgust she felt for the filthy street and the cramped dark house that was like a hutch, and the growing horror of spending her life there without change or escape, the feeling of misery produced by poverty, was all forgotten. The longing for a change of existence, of which she had first become dimly aware at the beginning of adolescence, when she had often cried herself to sleep for no tangible reason, was momentarily satisfied by the loveliness of spring.

Towards four o'clock she came upon a wood of young oak trees; she sat down there and felt that the day would remain imprinted on her mind for ever. She had never before seen the windflowers sweeping up from a hollow dark with wintry ivy leaves, modest, trembling, delicate things, white as if kissed by snow, dancing and quivering in the faint wind under the bare trees. Primroses in thousands, in clusters of pale yellow, were blooming shy and still among the stiff dark spears of unbudded hyacinth leaves. The wood was full of a trembling virgin light and the air was fragrant with the odour of the flowers and the promise of earth. The long, slender wands of a young ash-tree kept clapping together overhead with a restless sound. There was a pathway in the wood and presently she walked on, not touching the flowers, only gazing on them in a dreamy, bewildered way. But suddenly the possessive instinct of womanhood, the primitive need for beauty, made her fall to her knees and begin filling her hands. She gathered windflowers and primroses, bunching them separately, and then in a wide clear hollow of earth she found violets, heavily fragrant, dark and white. The purple flowers were solemn and mystic, and the white shone with a virgin purity, hanging discreet and lovely on their stems as the heads of nuns.

She went homeward at last with a sensation of intoxication, the beauty of the place sunk deep into her heart. It was late when she reached the street; tea was finished and Quintus had already gone off to spend his evening somewhere. She felt an overwhelming desire to talk of the wood to her mother and Fanny, but she said nothing and the wood remained something secret to her, like the first intimate communion with a lover.

Nevertheless she felt that she must speak. She felt as if ready to burst with fresh thoughts, new impressions, vague, unexpressed desires. She thought at last of Masher and went down the canal-path with a feeling that his presence was something necessary and vital to her, something without which she could not maintain the memory of the afternoon.

She came along the canal-path looking dreamily at the water and at the sky. At intervals she would take a quick, covert glance towards the brick-yard, but a clump of elders or a hedge of hawthorn would obscure her view and she would look away again with a mingling of relief and disappointment, trembling in a half-sad, half-delicious uncertainty. She did not see Masher until she had passed the elder-trees and had come to the open wooden fence skirting the field.

When she saw him half-way along the hawthorn hedge he was still setting potatoes. Involuntarily she stopped, leaned her arms on the fence and watched him. She felt impelled to watch him just as she had felt impelled to walk along the canal-path in order to see if he were there. His back was towards her. Now and then he stood upright, straightened his back and looked with a faint frown along the row of potatoes lying in the trench he had made. The trench was beautifully drawn and the potatoes made an even line, looking like pale eggs in the shadow. The plot was very orderly. In the more open ground there was a bed of daffodils, trembling and yellow, in full beauty, and then another of tulips, tall and stiff as drumsticks, their buds flushed with pink. Beyond this a line of currant-trees ended the plot and similar plots succeeded each other across the field to the walls of the brickyard. The soil in the field looked poor and yellowish. In the farthest corner a fire was pouring out white smoke that sailed languidly away over the clay-pit and the fields beyond.

Masher came to the end of the trench and uprooted the spit of his trenching line. He set it again a pace or two farther from the hedge and then walked along the trench in order to make it straight. He adjusted the other spit and walked back to fetch the bucket of potatoes and returned, swinging his free arm wide. The girl heard the clank of the bucket-handle. He spent a little time opening another trench. He worked methodically and with artistry, often looking critically back on the trench, his head a little to one side.

His presence, his movements, the mere fact of finding him there excited the girl. She did not take her eyes away from him, and when he took up the bucket again and began to drop in the potatoes, straddling along the row with feet wide apart, she followed his progress minutely, noted one by one the potatoes as they fell, critical and admiring of the line they made, and felt a strange pleasure when he finished and straightened his back again.

In a little while he began filling in the trenches. It was simple, dignified work; the pale soil crumbled over easily and the potatoes were buried quickly. With a sort of casual dignity he levelled off the ground, brought himself to rest on the pick-hoe, and lifted his eyes towards the brickyard as he rested.

Seeing this attitude Pauline recalled instantly the words he had spoken to her on the night when he carried up the oil for Adam. 'If there's one thing I'm sick and tired of more than another, it's that place. It's that which holds me down. I should have been gone long ago except for that.' They had talked together for a long time that evening in the dark yard after supper. Leaning with one hip against the water-barrel, wearing nothing but her indoor dress, she had sometimes bent her head to gaze at the sky and the stars mirrored perfectly in the black circle of water. His thoughts, his ideals, his quiet, principled manner of speaking had given her a thrill of pleasure. It had fired her imagination to hear the quietness of his speech shot with a murmur of passion, fiercely calculated, against the things he hated and which he held were wrong, unjust and unhappy. As he spoke to her of the injustice of things, the need to revolutionize a life blackened by poverty, filth, disease, sweating, prostitution, death, she had felt that every word was true, that not one accent had fallen out of place. She already knew enough of poverty for his words to have also a bitter significance for her. He defined her own unspoken ideals, the sad, bitter grievances which had sprung up with her youth. She felt that he understood the dark tortures and longings which she had suffered and could not express. He understood these things intuitively and for that reason she began to look up to him in a strange way, seeing no wrong in him. After this conversation in the darkness she thought of him a great deal and with timid expectation began to look for him wherever she went. His words repeated themselves in her mind, striking her intelligence afresh, and sometimes his face was evoked for her by a casual thought, and she was made inexplicably and almost unbearably conscious of a happiness hitherto unknown to her.

While she was thinking he finished off the ground with a few casual strokes of the pick-hoe and began to wind up the trenching line, criss-cross fashion, first on one spit, then on another. Having done this he went towards the hut, taking the hoe and line with him, disappearing for one moment and returning with empty hands to fetch the bucket and the potatoes.

Taking the bucket, swinging his free arm a little as

before, he again disappeared, and simultaneously she climbed through the fence and began to walk slowly along the hedge towards him.

Half-way along the hedge he reappeared and lifted a sack of potatoes and hoisted it over his back. He had not taken two steps before he saw her. Without another step forward he lowered the potato-sack from his shoulder and waited for her to come.

She began explaining, hastily, her self-consciousness a pain to her, that she had come to buy flowers for Fanny to put on her husband's grave. The excuse, rising to her lips on the moment, made her feel ashamed. He smiled. She was reassured by this smile and by the words he spoke to her:

'You have come in time for the daffodils.'

'The daffodils are lovely,' she said. 'They shine a long way off.'

'The wallflowers are out too,' he said. 'They look well together. Come over. I'll show them to you.'

She hesitated but he waved his hand in the direction of the currant-trees and moved away. She followed without a word, catching the faint, half-sweet, half-sourish odour of the daffodils and then the rich fragrance of the hidden wallflowers, very beautiful, powerful and soft as velvet in the air. She followed him closely and suddenly he stopped and she could see the closely branching wallflowers in a long bed, their blossoms tawny and blackish crimson in the dusk with faint yellow plants interspersed here and there, the pale flowers like sleepy eyes turned upwards.

As they stood side by side gazing at the flowers she was aware of a peculiar happiness. The flowers, which had been all her life like daisies, common and accepted and half-noticed things, became suddenly very beautiful and significant of something new.

'Let me get you some,' he said.

59

He bent down on one knee and she heard the snap of first one brittle stalk, then another and another. He worked gradually up the bed, breaking the stems with his left hand and holding the bunch awkwardly against his breast with his right.

'It's misty over against the clay-pit,' she said, looking across the field, 'or is it smoke?'

'That's mist now. It'll be there when I go on in the morning.'

'What time do you go on?'

'Six o'clock.'

'We go in at half-past seven,' she said, 'and that's a job.'

'In the summer I sometimes come down here and do a little hoeing or something and bring my breakfast. You work at Joyce's don't you?'

'Yes,' she said.

He straightened his back and ran his fingers among the stalks of flowers, frilling out leaves and blossoms and glancing covertly at her.

'What do you do?'

'Skiving and on the machine,' she said.

'What's it like there?'

'I put up with it.'

'What's the trouble?'

'The place is too old and we're crowded in, and you've got to lick the fore-woman's hand before you get anything. It's rotten work too, all cheap and ironed and polished up to look what it isn't.'

'I know.'

'The old man comes in and swears at us when the stuff isn't good.'

'As if it's your fault! He's a swine. I knew Joyce when he lived in a house no bigger than that of yours and his children hadn't a rag to their backs and he was glad to pawn his watch. Some people are born pigs and money

60

can't alter them. He'll be a pig right up to his coffin, that man.'

They gradually walked away from the bed of wall-flowers as he talked and came back to the daffodils. A dusk was creeping over the field, rapidly and almost imperceptibly deepening, so that the yellow trumpets of the flowers seemed sometimes to be floating stemless above a bed of green. He bent down in silence and as before began slowly working up the bed, breaking the stalks with his left hand. Here and there shone a few star-like narcissi, frail and virgin white, with the pheasants' eyes turned to black in the dusk, and he would every now and then gather a single one, disturbing its fragrance, and put it more tenderly with the rest. There was pleasure for her in watching all this; she dwelt by turns on the bend of his head, his black hair, and more often, instinctively, on his hands, the short, strong fingers that crooked about the slender stems, broke them cleanly and folded about the enlarging bunch. There were moments when her eyes opened wide and she lapsed into a dreamy state of thought from which some sound of his or a sudden rush of fragrance from the flowers would arouse her with a start. He worked to the end of the bed and returned, stepping across it, planting his feet carefully among the yellow clumps and choosing at intervals some lovelier blossom that caught his fancy.

She lost her confusion while watching him and an assurance springing from delight took its place, but the confusion returned when he ceased gathering the flowers.

'They look pretty together,' he said.

He gave them to her and without thinking she took them, thrust her face down to them and said:

'They're lovely. How much for them?'

'Nothing.'

He turned his back and began walking in the direction of the hut. His voice was abrupt.

'But these are for Fanny, for the grave. I'll buy them.'

'Nothing.'

She walked up the path behind him, a little guilty and at a loss.

'I knew Jimmie,' she heard him say. 'Put them there for me. It's all the same really. When is it coming, by the way, that baby?'

'In June, that's what we think. She don't know herself, hardly.'

'She don't know?' he repeated.

'She don't want it. It don't mean much to her. That's the trouble.'

He nodded his head and was silent, in understanding.

A moment later he reached the hut; he stooped and propped open the door a little wider. Then he went inside and came out again quickly, holding a blue can in his hands.

'There's some tea,' he said.

'No thank you.'

'It's cold, but I could warm it on the oil-stove. It'll be thrown away if you don't drink it.'

She hated the thought of its being wasted.

'Shall I put it on?' he said.

She nodded her head and he returned to the hut with the can. 'Come in,' she heard him say.

The hut was very small. Masher began to fumble with matches. He struck one and she saw a little oil-stove standing on a rough wooden table. Laying down the flowers in the damp grass growing by the side of the hut she entered; the oil-stove was beginning to burn and she saw a chair without a back, a few sacks and a heap of tools in one corner, and then along one wall bunches of drying seed stalks tied in white paper bags, and an old calendar. An old shot-gun was hanging upon another wall, above a little square window curtained with spiders' webs. Presently

Masher turned up the oil-stove, closed it and put on the tea-can. The stove smoked, and mingled with the smell of oil was a dry odour of old earth, a breath of mice and cobwebs. It was difficult to move about and she sat down on a sack of potatoes. There was a sensation of comfort in her limbs as she sat down, and looking through the doorway she pondered with pleasure for a moment or two over the narrow view over the darkening field, the white mist and the chimneys rising like immense black candles against the sky.

Masher found a tea-cup and a blue tin mug coloured with fresh tea stains; he set the mug aside for himself but the cup he washed out with a little warm tea, rinsing it rapidly round and round and hurling the dregs through the doorway. Soon there was a noise in the tea-can and he turned out the stove. The tea steamed and hissed as it was poured out. There was a full cup for Pauline and he drained a little for himself, colouring the bottom of the mug a pale brown.

They sat for a few minutes in silence, drinking the tea. A thrush sat singing in the hawthorn-hedge, a little distance away, lost in ecstasy.

'I saw you off to church on Easter Sunday,' said Masher at last. 'You and that little sweater. Do you often go?'

'We sometimes go together,' she said.

'Do you believe in it?' he asked.

'Why shouldn't I believe?'

'What is it you believe anyway?'

'I believe it's right and I believe in God,' she said.

They were silent for a little while; and then he said:

'Do you believe there was a Christ?'

'Yes,' she said.

The thrush was still singing. Things were dim in the hut and over the field beyond.

'Who was Christ?' he said to her.

'The Son of the Virgin Mary of course.'

'Virgin!' he caught up the word. 'You know what that means?'

'Yes.'

'His mother was a virgin. No one had touched her. You know what it means?'

'Yes.'

'She was a mother and a virgin. It's nonsense. It's all wrong. How could it be? How could it? You know that. And that's what I used to ask myself. I never straightened things after I stumbled on that. I used to ask myself why I didn't believe—and then I found out that and I knew. It was all a sham—humbug—rotten at the base. Pah! People put their trust in Christianity because they hope for one thing in return.'

'What thing?'

'Forgiveness of sins. That's all. That's where Christ differs from all the rest. That's His trump card.'

'Supposing we'd never been promised forgiveness of sins?' said the girl, half-shocked by these words.

'A sin is a sin, whether you forgive it or not!' he said fiercely.

'Yet it would be queer sometimes not to forgive,' she said, 'don't you think so?'

'Then let's forgive each other,' he said quickly, 'not wait to be forgiven. Perhaps Christ meant that. I don't know. If you understand you forgive, naturally. But how often do we understand?'

A peewit had begun to cry over the field and the thrush could no longer be heard. Slowly and pensively the girl took a drink of the warm tea and as she drank she felt that the words 'How often do we understand?' seemed to float round and round in her mind. The words themselves were arresting and a little melancholy.

'Why do we talk like this?' she said.

'Conversation starts itself and goes on and there it is.'

'If I talk to you much longer I shall be frightened,' she said.

'Frightened of what? Only frightened of your own ignorance,' he told her. 'It's the unknown that make us frightened.'

'I don't like it.'

'What don't you like?'

'I don't like what you say about Jesus Christ and forgiveness and God.'

'Have I been moralizing?'

'It fills my head with all sorts of ideas until I don't know what to think.'

'Do you want to go?' he said.

She did not at once reply and he swung himself off the table where he had been sitting and went to the door and she heard him say:

'I don't often get moralizing.'

The tea was growing cold and she drank the last of it in a sudden gulp and followed him outside. He had moved away from the door and was standing a little distance off, by the bed of daffodils.

'I ought to gather a few,' he said as she came up.

'Don't you want to gather them?' she asked. The tone of his voice was full of regret.

'I hate it,' he said. 'Flowers ought to grow and die and not be gathered.'

He stood for a moment contemplating the dim rows of flowers. It was suddenly very still over the field, with not even the faintest stirring in the grass, the daffodils colourless as ghosts, the wallflowers blackened and dissolved into the earth's darkness, and the earth itself asleep. The air was cool but the fragrance of the flowers floated up warmly and softly.

He suddenly bent down and as before she heard the

dull snap of a stem. He straightened his back and held up a daffodil.

'They used to teach me at school,' he said, 'which were the stamens and which was the calyx and which was the ovary and so on. But I've forgotten. I don't know and I don't care now. You don't need to know anatomy before you can tell when you see a beautiful woman. You know that all right. And that's how it is with this daffodil. I know it's beautiful and that's all I want to know.'

His voice was low and ran on carelessly, as if he were speaking to himself.

'I ought to gather a few,' he said.

'For the shop?' she asked.

He nodded and turned suddenly to her and spoke with conscious heat.

'And there's another thing. We sell them. You'd have thought that in Charlotte's Row and round about nobody would find the money to buy flowers. But that's how it is with the poor. They're uneducated, and uneducated folks are always superstitious, and the poor spend as much on satisfying their superstitions as would buy books to educate them. It's a circle—the old vicious circle, if you like. I put the daffodils into the earth, they flower, I gather them, my missus sells them, the daffodils go to the graves and back to the earth again, and with the money we get we buy a few more daffodils for another spring, and by another spring a few more folks are dead. And so it goes on. You and me go to work and earn money to keep ourselves alive so as we can go to work. It's beautiful, isn't it? Isn't it a noble way of going on?'

She felt the bitterness in his voice, and the hopeless irony of his words hurt and bewildered her. With a sudden rush of feeling she found herself pitying him. She pondered confusedly over his words and the pessimism underlying them, asking herself repeatedly why he should talk thus, but she hardly understood, and only her pity resolved itself, warming her heart, filling her with an acute tenderness and connecting, in some way, her mind with his. This pity seemed also to make him suddenly attractive and she found herself half-consciously going over the details of his face, the dark eyes, the knotty forehead, the thin brown cheeks, the lips, the chin, before he bent down and began hastily snatching off, as if impatiently, stalk after stalk of daffodils.

There was displeasure in all his movements; she heard the juicy stems crunch under his fingers, the leaves torn and the angry rustle of the blossoms gathered up into an untidy bunch.

When he had gathered the bunch and they had returned to the hut and she had picked up her own flowers, he said:

'If I didn't gather them and it rained, the rain would ruin them. If it was hot they'd be blown and dead in a day.'

She held the flowers for him while he padlocked the door. The stems were torn and shiny with sap and the bunch ill-made. She carried both his bunch and her own until they reached the canal, and then he took his own, gripping the bunch awkwardly and swinging it at his side with indifference, brushing the flower heads alternately against himself and against her skirt.

A train came out of the distance with an increasing roar, going southward. The carriages were flooded with light and the furnace shot a red beam far up into the darkening sky.

They stood still. The train thundered past and vanished and they heard it tearing furiously past the town, shrieking intermittently.

'Come up to Madox's top room and have something to drink,' he said when it was silent again.

'They don't open Sundays.'

'They do now.'

'I don't think I'll come.'

'They have a man on the piano there now and a girl on a mandoline.'

'I don't think I'll come.'

There was a note of unhappiness in his voice and she wanted suddenly to ask him why he was unhappy, why he had begun to speak dejectedly, and then why he walked on without speaking at all. These things began to concern her deeply, but she kept silent, shy and hesitant and feeling also that he was hardly known to her.

They walked under the railway-bridge and into Charlotte's Row, and troubled by the silence into which her refusal had plunged them, she said:

'Who goes to Madox's? A lot of socialists?'

'Not many socialists.'

'I'd like to go up one evening, but not to-night.'

'I should like to take you,' he said.

They stood a little while beyond the railway-bridge, talking of unimportant things, and then casually he picked out another daffodil, and then another and another, until there were five, and gave them to her. His hands moved casually and slowly, without excitement, as if all this hardly mattered to him. The girl, however, was trembling and excited. The act was something extraordinary and precious to her, and the remembrance of it would not let her rest. She afterwards conjured dreamy, improbable, exciting thoughts about it and the significance of it grew in her mind and established itself there, as though for ever.

CHAPTER V

ON Sunday evenings Adam and his grandmother would
go to visit the old woman's sister-in-law on the far side of
the town, walking slowly through dozens of streets similar
to that in which they lived before reaching their destina-
tion. It was always very dirty in the streets and there
would be groups of loungers waiting for the public-houses
to open at every corner and children playing at hop-scotch
on the narrow pavements under the sordid windows. Mrs.
Hosking would be dressed in black, and two blood-ripe
cherries would everlastingly bob and dance on the brim
of her black hat, and a little delicate silver reindeer would
gently leap on its chain across the black silk of her breast
as she walked along. She always carried, too, an umbrella,
a little patent leather black bag and a box of peppermints.
The sweets were to be eaten as they walked along; the bag
was for use when they returned.

After a long time they would reach a house which stood
on a high causeway. There was a silver fish as large as a
salmon dangling from a line over the door, turning whenever the wind struck it as if it were swimming in the air.
Beneath this sign was a window full of fishing rods and
boxes of hooks and many floats of the brightest green and
crimson, and in the centre of the window was a second
fish, in a glass case, stuffed and poised in imaginary blue
water among drab green weeds. Above this stood a photo-
graph of a man with a big moustache who was holding up
a string of dozens of fish with an air of stupid triumph on
his face, so that he himself looked curiously like a fish too.

Mrs. Hosking would knock on the door and presently

there would be a shuffling sound of feet and someone would draw back the bolts. Slowly the door would begin to open, gradually a yellowish face would appear, and a woman's voice, very old and almost inarticulate, would say in a whisper:

'You can come in.'

Adam would follow his grandmother into the shop. It was always very shadowy in the shop and there was a smell of dust and mice and camphor. From every side birds and animals and myriads of butterflies seemed to be looking down upon him from glass cases. Over the doorway leading to the rear of the shop hung an otter biting its little white fangs into a fish, and there was a fox in another case which stood red and beautiful and alert, as if scenting the presence of man. The butterflies were magically beautiful; they were pinned into cases shaped like diamonds and the cases were painted inside a soft blue like a summer sky; the dead wings were unfaded and faultless and there was a lightness and grace about them that made it difficult to believe that they were dead. There were many cases of beetles and flies, curious creatures pinned in rows of exquisite symmetry. In the dim room they had no colour and the boy's gaze never lingered over them but travelled always quickly back to the butterflies. There were butterflies as large as his hand and others as small and frail as the petals of a primrose. Their wings were coloured in sulphur and crimson, or in a dusty blue like the hue of a flax-bloom, or they would be patterned in with tortoise-shell or hang from their pins like autumn leaves, soft and brown, the damask of their bloom a rich and unfingered loveliness.

In the dark and pokey room behind the shop there were other butterflies and birds, and in this room the two women and the boy would sit at an old round table with a pedestal leg and drink tea. Even after the tea-pot had

70

been drained quite dry the women would sit over the empty tea-cups and continue talking. The woman was very tall and angular, with steel-grey hair brushed straight back from her bony yellow forehead, and her head quivered from side to side like a poplar leaf as she talked.

The talk was very often involved and concerned things he did not understand, but occasionally as he sat staring at the cases of flies and birds hanging on the walls he heard his own name. Whenever this happened he noticed also that they began to talk of a woman and he gathered that she had been young and beautiful and that something terrible had once happened to her. Once as they were talking of her his grandmother asked him suddenly to stand up in the light of the window. He stood up and the two women scrutinized him and when he sat down again he heard them say:

'Yes, he is like her about the eyes and the mouth. He is just like her.'

He heard of her many times and he began to understand at last that she was his mother. He had never known his mother and he longed desperately to ask if this were her, why they talked of her, what terrible thing she had done and most of all where she had gone? Each time he felt he must ask, however, a lump like a frog came into his throat and a strange uneasiness allied to melancholy kept him dumb.

All these conversations became full of significance for him; he was attracted constantly, in a mysterious way, to the thought of his mother. One wet spring evening, as he sat in the kitchen with Pauline, making a peep-show from a white boot-box that the girl had found, his mind was full of the thought of her, his curiosity complex and sad as he made peep-holes in the sides of the box with a steel and watched the girl creating a panorama of pictures cut from the pages of an old fashion magazine. The blank wall that

71

ended the row made the kitchen gloomy. The rain falling steadily outside ran slowly down the wall, dripping regularly in fat drops from the window. The boy had mixed a flour-paste in a saucer, and the bare table was strewn with bright-coloured fragments of paper; the pictures were of women's heads, a lovely bright-skinned country girl carrying a basket of gooseberries, a girl in a wedding-dress and a picture of what Pauline said was a countess riding to hounds, stiffly attired in a black habit and a man's bowler hat, riding side-saddle on a chestnut horse with a white nose. These were pasted on the longer sides of the box; for the ends of the box they were still to cut out subjects, and the boy had fixed his mind on finding a man fishing and a bird as lovely as those hanging in the shop to which he and his grandmother walked on Sundays.

He paused at intervals over the page of another magazine and looked up and spoke to her.

'There's a fish hanging outside on a line. Haven't you ever been?' he said. 'It's a long way. And there's a lot more fish, some in the window and more inside and animals and birds staring at you. Every time you look you see something you didn't see before. And then the butterflies. Some bigger than my hand and some not so big as that little locket granny wears. Granny says all our family were butterfly-catchers and fishermen. They didn't work for their living, like other folks. That's how they've always been.'

'Can you find a bird?'

'Not yet.' His heart suddenly began to pound in his throat and he was troubled. 'Did my mother,' he said, 'like birds and butterflies?'

'I don't know. I fancy so. I fancy she must have done,' the girl said softly. 'I fancy so.'

'Did you know her?'

'I can remember her.'

'Where is she now?'

'She's not here any longer.'

He paused, detecting the uneasiness in her voice, and said quietly:

'Is she dead?'

'Yes, she's dead,' she answered softly.

For a moment he was silent.

There were no birds in the pages of the book he had been turning over.

'Why is she dead?' he asked.

'Her heart broke,' she said.

'She couldn't live any longer after her heart broke,' said the boy.

'No.'

'Why did it break?'

The girl pasted the back of the countess riding to hounds and pressed her with trembling fingers to the white interior of the box and said:

'A man made her unhappy and things didn't come right for her.'

'Why did he make her unhappy?'

Pauline took the picture of the girl in the wedding-dress and pasted in that also and said:

'She liked him very much and she could see no wrong in him.'

'Was there any wrong in him?'

'He went away and left her. He was older than her and things were never the same for him as they were for her. She gave up everything.'

'Why did she give up everything?'

He was looking at her fixedly and the insistence of his glance was such that she felt troubled and tried to escape it. She stirred the paste with her fore-finger and wiped her finger on a scrap of paper and repeated:

'She could see no wrong in him.'

73

Under a pretence of looking at the rain the girl went to the window and stood there briefly, cutting meticulously round the head of a Roman consul she had found. There was a long silence and the boy seemed to accept this silence unconsciously, trying to disentangle in his own mind the things the girl had related, troubled by the inexplicable sense of something tragic in her words and the fear in her voice. Upon certain phrases and more especially upon the phrase 'She could see no wrong in him,' his mind pondered restlessly, astounded by the immensity of such devotion and a little intimidated by the thought of such beauty. Trying to envisage her face he saw his mother as pale and very beautiful and he was conscious of a pride in her that was more powerful than his sadness. He turned over the leaves of the book while thinking of her and presently he came upon the picture of an eagle, black and terrible, and before the picture of the eagle the picture of his mother gradually retreated, sinking deep in his mind and making an everlasting impression there.

Pauline finished the head of the consul and went back to the table to begin to cut out the eagle. It was difficult to steer the scissors among the feathers, and the talons were difficult also. While she was doing this Adam, with a little red paint, decorated the interior of the box with red curtains, painted at each corner, draped back like the curtains at a theatre when the performance has begun.

He worked quickly, full of excitement, anxious to see the end. She was more patient and he urged her continually with eager cries:

'Hurry, you're so slow. We shan't finish till bull's noon.'

'You want this eagle to look proper, don't you?'

'Yes, but hurry. Folks are waiting to peep.'

'If we do hurry we can't get done to-night.'

'Why not? Why can't we get done?'

'I've got to go out somewhere.'

A quiver of disappointment ran through him but he did not speak.

'You can go and sit with the lodgers until granny comes,' she said. 'You know you can always go. Or you can go and stay with my mother a bit.'

'I didn't know you had to go.'

There was a criticism in the faintly regretful, detached tone of his voice, and she detected a shadow of anger in his face as he bent over the box and painted in dead silence with sullen and ill-directed sweeps of his brush, making the curtains ragged and spilling the paint on the white cardboard floor of the show.

'I must go,' she said.

'When must you go?'

'When you've painted the curtains and we've pasted this eagle I think I ought to go.'

In the ensuing silence, as he daubed with sullen reck-lessness he seemed to ignore her, paying a perfunctory attention to her repeated assurances that she would help him to finish to-morrow, and when she bent over him he half-stiffened himself against her.

The curtain was finished at last, he washed his brush at the sink and she pasted in the eagle with supreme care. She waited a little and then began to pack up the coloured scraps, the paste and the scissored magazines with the half-finished show, repeatedly promising that she would come again to-morrow, but he only listened to her moodily, helping her half-heartedly, all his gaiety and insistence gone.

Thereafter he was often made wretched by a remem-brance of the girl's words about his mother; his misery was strange and hard, and he was conscious always of being awed by something unknown and exquisite, as by an image too perfect ever to attain. At times there was a sense of loss in him so heavy that the thought of tears would be crushed, and at others a sense of such vague, illimitable, bitter confusion, like a curious pain, that his heart seemed to be squeezed with intolerable agony, until he felt it sicken and faint away in his breast, weeping like some small timid beast trapped in the clutch of a powerful hand.

Going off with his grandmother across the town one evening in May he returned with a fishing-rod and some hooks and a little red float that the old woman had given him. 'You may as well take it and be a fisherman like the others have been,' she said. 'All your family were fishermen, every one of them. I used to weep my eyes sore wondering where Eli had gone, going away in the morning and not showing his face till dark again. When he could fish that man would never work, and when he was working he was never happy till he was fishing again. You spring from a lazy lot, my boy. A lazy, dreamy, good-for-nothing, soft-hearted lot, that's what you spring from. Take Eli. He couldn't live without the river and the woods. He wasn't happy unless he was sitting on a river-bank, or nosing about with a lantern for some moth he wanted. Six nights out of seven I used to fall asleep afore he came upstairs. And that's how they've all been. Butterflies and birds, flowers and fishing, that made them happy. Look at Rook. He was your great-uncle. He didn't know Rook perhaps, did he Maria? Well, he was another. He could fish better than any man who ever breathed. Yes, that man had secrets that the gentry would have given any amount for. He knew where the best fish lay, he knew how to catch them, he knew everything. And no more common sense than this table-leg. Not so much, in fact. That's what he was like. He'd catch fish and sell them for a copper without thinking. Yes, you spring from a fine lot. Rook's wife ran away with a lodger and left him without a penny, but even that never woke him, the silly toad. You

76

never knew him. A big tall man with a beard and top-boots. You'd have known him the moment you set eyes on him.'

The news of his relations enthralled the boy and the fishing-rod became very precious. He lay in bed on the warm evenings that followed and felt that he too desired a life like the life of Rook and Eli. Staring at the dirty ceiling of the room he saw himself on the banks of a stream, the day sultrily warm, the sky blue and clear as a bead of glass, the water itself without a ripple and the shadows of willows meeting the willows themselves in the smooth pool. He would fancy himself beginning to fish under the trees, knowing nothing of what to do except that he must put a worm on the hook and cast the hook to the water and that he must be silent, not moving or speaking when once the float was at rest; and in imagination and also in dreamy actuality he would keep still, the perfect form of the summer day as motionless before his eyes as if painted. And by and by, when he had endured suspense enough, the fish would steer from under the willow-roots or the green reeds into the sun-steeped water, greyish in colour or a dull silver brushed with red, and roam with slow grace in and out of the shadows or lie mysteriously on the pale sand without a movement, as if sleeping. Little troops of fish would emerge into the sunlight and vanish into the dark regions of the stream, and some bigger fish would thresh the water, as if angry, showing its silver belly in the bright depths; a fly would touch the pool, making unending rings, and soon, with the water at rest and transparent again and the afternoon sunk into a deep languor, his fish would come. It would be fat and handsome, flecked with red, and his heart would pound as the fish came for the bait and he saw the float plunge. In his excitement he would know nothing of how the fish came from the water; it would merely thresh and leap a little in the grass but finally he would close his hand over its cold squirming shape until it died. After the first bite it was easier to fish and he would pull in the line again and again, more and more greedily, the details of the day fading a little in his mind against his passion to possess. Very shortly the day would fade entirely, the water swooning away, and great fish would swim drunkenly to and fro before his eyes until he slept.

He thought a great deal of life as his family had led it, asking his grandmother questions, and he wished also to be free. Rivers, birds, woods, fishes became emblems of another existence in which Charlotte's Row, the hot dustiness of the yards, the shabby gardens, the factories and drumming machines had no place. At times he was disturbed by these desires into a remembrance of what had taken place on the evening when the old lady had pressed her dry wrinkled lips on his and had given him the fishing-rod. That evening the journey home had been very slow. His grandmother seemed to walk with greater difficulty and her breath came in short gasps, and often with the faintest squeaking, as if she had a toy whistle under her lips. He often carried the bag and his grandmother often leant against the wall, overtaken by a fit of coughing. She coughed with a metallic, rasping sound in her chest and her face was sometimes blue when the coughing ended. After that she would spit continually and fetch great sighs, as if the journey and the coughing had exhausted her.

The boy was troubled afterwards by the blue of her face. Lying in bed he knew very well that she was ill and it was difficult to rid himself of the thought that she might die. The thought made him solemnly afraid, for he could not imagine what he would do, or what his life would be like if ever she were to die.

He lay awake and while she was undressing in the candle light, grunting and puffing a little as she unloosed

78

her stays and laid aside her petticoats on a chair, he said to her naïvely :

'Don't die. You musn't die.'

She uttered something very low in answer to him, but what it was he never knew. He only remembered for ever her sobbing and the rain of sudden tears which rolled soundlessly down her cheeks like little hard white stones in the candlelight.

CHAPTER VI

THE Harpers were very proud and fond of display and were never happy except when living beyond their means. 'Harpers,' their neighbours said, 'they like to think they're a notch above a tapper.' In their desire to outshine their neighbours and their zeal to keep up an appearance of being better, they were like some family of poor aristocracy. Money was nothing; they could live eternally on credit; or it was easy to run and see Bernstein, the pawnbroker; or it was easier still to borrow half a loaf, or a copper for the gas-meter, or a handful of raisins and forget conveniently ever to pay them back again. And so Quintus could drink and strut like a peacock, and the two youngest sons could dress like dandies and appeared flashily at clubs and Saturday evening dances. They kept expensive dogs and rubbed elbows with all the pseudo sporting gentry at dog-races for forty miles round. Display was everything. Their dogs must run fastest; they must own a gramophone with a larger horn and a louder tone than the people two doors away. They bragged incessantly of what they had; and those things that were for some reason out of their pockets' reach were nothing, or they had owned them long since and had long since forgotten them. There was often a sneering note in their pride and they were great liars.

They were unusually poor about the time of Pauline's twenty-first birthday. Summer was coming on and there was little work for Quintus.

'You might make a pair or two,' said his wife, 'and put them by until winter-time, for when things'll be better. But I might as soon talk to a dead horse as talk to you!'

80

And as though to prove her words he would slink away with his dog on the first warm morning, with a piece of bread and meat in his pocket, and prowl along the hedge rows of the fields, peeping for nests, or sit smoking in the shade of a wood of bluebells, or lie on his back in a meadow with a cowslip in his mouth, indolent and happy, listening to the skylarks singing as they climbed infinitely above him in the golden light.

Nevertheless, though they were poor, Pauline must have her party. To the Harpers it would have been unthinkable not to celebrate her birthday. And Pauline, though she hated and despised the endless credit and borrowing and lying, had looked forward to the party also. She had saved a little money. And she was very happy, baking the birthday-cake in readiness and covering it with icing, so that it shone white as frozen snow, and dreaming vaguely of the twenty-one candles, each with its tiny orange flame on the waxen green stem, burning up from the white cake like a ring of crocuses.

The party took its shape definitely in her mind. She worked out the details, chose the guests, wondered how many people could crowd into the tiny living-room. There would be singing, games, plenty of eating. She invited her Uncle Jude, who would bring his viola. There would be the gramophone. Jude was frail, white-haired, a little eccentric, and he would weep if they forgot to ask him to play, and then weep with joy over his own tunes when they remembered. She would decorate the rooms, have many jars of bluebells, ask her father to bring home cowslips. The place would be gay, spring-like, quite transformed. There would be a special place for the cake to stand so that no one should miss the sight of it: the virgin whiteness, the pattern of silver fern-leaves along the rim, the soft green candles.

She talked of it with her mother. It appeared then that

there were people she had forgotten, her father's people, old friends of her mother's, people who would be offended.

'Put them down, girl! What are you hesitating for? You're only twenty-one once.'

'Let 'em all come!' said Quintus.

She had dreamed of a modest party, beautiful, quiet, very happy. Now Quintus was insisting on his friends, men she detested or did not even know. She wrote them down with an increasing wretchedness, knowing they would come whether she wished it or not. Every day he managed to remember some fresh name.

'Put China Williams down. I forgot old China.'

'*That* man!' she cried. 'Not if I never have a party at all!'

'Here, put him down, I tell you! What's the matter with you? Ain't he good enough for you?'

'We'll have no street-touts in this house!' she said vehemently.

'In this house, eh?' he sneered. 'How many folks do you think are coming to poke the'selves in this house?'

'As many as I want. And those who don't like it can stay away.'

He looked contemptuously at the little room, where every stick of furniture was crowded against another. She looked at it too, at the broken-down sofa, the heavy treadle sewing-machine, the scanty little table hardly big enough for a game of cards.

'I suppose you think you can squeeze eighty-odd folks in here?' he asked.

'Eighty! Who said there were eighty? Don't get that into your head.'

'There'll be as near eighty as nick it, my gal.'

'Not if I know it!'

'By God! You want a party, don't you, not a peep-show?'

82

'I want nothing now,' she said. 'I'll have no party.'

'You're just at that damn-fool age!' he shouted, 'when you don't know what you do want!'

'I know enough to know that I want no party now.'

She was proud and miserable. He incessantly sneered at her. Weren't his friends good enough for her? Was she afraid they were going to upset the little prayer-meeting in the parlour? What the devil was the matter with her lately? There was no peace between them. And then in one of their quarrels it came out that he had ordered a room for the party, a room that would hold the eighty guests in comfort.

She was furious. 'Where? Where?' she demanded. 'Where is this room?'

It turned out to be a room over the old posting-stable behind *The Angel*, his favourite pub. It was very large, they could hire the crockery, there was a piano.

'Some sense of a room!' he declared. 'There you'll be able to have a party worth having.'

'I daresay! And who's going to pay for it?'

'What do you think I ordered the room for? The room'll be paid for. Get that out of your head!'

'Very well,' she said, 'as long as we have some understanding.'

There was nothing she could do. She felt defeated. She resigned herself to the room over the stable, the eighty guests, the miserable sham and pretence of it all. The Harpers on the other hand were delighted. They boasted incessantly, lied fabulously. 'There's going to be fiddle and a piano for dancing and a man a-conjuring and Pauline has a dress that was made for an actress.'

On the day itself she wore a dress of peacock-green; the fine, bright-coloured silk was drawn tight like a sheaf over her young round breasts and her waist; the rich, lustred colour matched her darkness and pallor handsomely. The dress was her own work. She was proud and happy.

She nursed in her heart again the feeling that everything would be well, the party after all very happy. There was great excitement. Quantities of cakes and tarts had been made, there were enormous pink hams. Her father had brought home sheaves of cowslips; the sweet, lusty, golden heads of bloom softened her heart and made her forget her bitterness. And taking the basket of cowslips in order to decorate the room she found miraculously that she liked the place. She loved suddenly its clean, whitewashed walls, its spaciousness, its canopy of dark oak rafters. The long wooden tables stretching the length of the room suggested some banquet. The windows were long casements, high up, which let in draughts of the fresh, summer-morning air, the odour of straw, the faint, indefinable smell of horses from the stables in the yard below. There were cowslips enough to decorate the tables. She half closed her eyes, and looked fondly on the splashes of warm gold and dreamed with happiness.

As she stood there she heard footsteps, small and soft, climbing the ladder from below. She waited. And presently Adam appeared, dressed in his coarse cloth Sunday jacket and corduroys and heavy black boots, ready for the party. He looked painfully solemn and old, much older than his years. His arms were full of sprays of may-blossom, crimson and white, heavy as guelder-roses, the red like a gay and beautiful blush against the wild, virgin white, and the scent of it sickly and faint.

She stared. Her eyes shone with pleasure. He looked so small and awkward, so painfully in earnest. The prolific load of blossoms weighed him down. Coming into the room he tried to remove his cap; he failed sadly, the sprays of bloom dropping to the floor, powdering the air with the pinkish dust of their myriads of stamens.

84

At last he let fall a heavy crimson spray. Trying desperately to recover it he knocked off his cap. She ran to him at once, overjoyed, and kissed his white, astonished face through the veil of blossoms.

'Heaven knows where you found such may! And the pink! I tell you, Heaven only knows.'

Her kiss had made him more than ever shy, solemn and confused.

'Granny says it's unlucky,' he said.

'That's an old grandmother's tale! Just like any old grandmother.'

'She bundled me out of the house with it.'

'But it's fine, the finest may I ever saw, the finest ever. What tales!'

Together they found a tall stone jar, arranged the may-blossom, and stood for many minutes in admiration of the gay festoons of the red flaunting themselves over the dreamy heads of the white.

In the evening the may was still fresh and beautiful. And the party, after all, seemed as if it would go beautifully too. The room was crowded, people were shouting and laughing, she was very excited. Her father had dressed himself up as she had never seen him: a brown tweed suit, a starched white collar, a stiff, blazing white dicky and white tie. His black hair was beautifully brushed; a wisp of it was pressed over his forehead in a shining curve, like a black sickle. He looked very handsome, she thought, and striking, with the early yellow rosebud in his coat. He welcomed people boisterously, shouted stentoriously across the room, and after tea made foolish, lovable speeches about her; the eighty guests stamped their feet and tinkled the spoons in their tea-cups and banged the tables with delight.

The piles of cakes were in ruins, the bone was already gleaming bare and white on the hams. Pauline sat pale, a little scared, but happy, staring alternately at the red and white blossoms of hawthorn and at the shining white cake with its ring of soft green candles burning with flickering golden light.

When darkness began to fall the old brass gas-chandelier hanging from the roof was lighted. The gas-jets burned with naked light, giving a golden glow which fell murkily on the faces of the guests dancing, the hot-looking man in evening dress at the piano, the fluttery dresses of the women. The room was stifling, there seemed hundreds of whirling figures. Quintus sailed among them with a woman on his arm, proud and steady as some old schooner. The girl saw her younger brothers dancing with two little dolls, strangers to her, painted like bits of china, with sinuous bodies writhing under scarlet and yellow dresses.

There were many people she did not know. The room was full of strangers. One by one her father's cronies were drifting in. The memory of the party she had planned rose up in her. She slipped out into the yard below for a breath of air. She felt her excitement gradually being dissipated.

As she was going downstairs a boy with a white apron was coming up. He stopped her.

'Where shall I put the wine?' he said.

'The wine? What wine?'

'It was ordered,' he said.

'Not for this party.'

He showed her his basket. Dark necks of wine-bottles were plainly visible at the foot of the stairs. She went down and looked at them.

'Half a dozen port, half a dozen claret, two Burgundies, two bottles of whisky,' he said.

She stared at them, she saw her name plainly on the ticket of delivery.

'Take them up,' she said.

86

She went upstairs again. The dancing was in full swing, but a group of men, urged on by her father, were already at the wine like bees. She wandered about the room, sick with apprehension.

She stood by the piano and watched the dancers and pretended she was supervising it all. The hammers clanged and jangled, the purple cloth at the back of the piano quivered. Her uncle Jude, with his viola ready in his hands, was standing at the piano also, waiting to be asked to play. He was trembling violently, like a child.

He looked at her with simple, pathetic blue eyes, ready to weep. At one time he had been a beautiful player. Drink and epilepsy had ruined him. Now he was foolish, white-haired—a wreck of his former self, though he fancied that he could play beautifully still.

She spoke to him.

'You can play for dancing?' she said.

His eyes shone with tears. He tried to master himself, but big tears rolled helplessly down his cheeks. In spite of this, like a true Harper, he managed in some way to put into his voice a hint of something boastful.

'I used to play at all the big houses,' he quavered. 'I've been to play for the Marquis of Exeter. I've played everywhere. Good viola-players are scarce. But nowadays they don't know that, they don't know that. They don't want me to play.'

'You shall play,' she said. 'You shall play. Don't go crying.'

Presently he became calm, picked out his music and dusted his viola.

'What can you play, Judy?' said the man on the piano.

'Shall we play *The Blue Danube*?'

'Sure your fingers won't crack?'

'I played it once,' he said proudly, 'for a duke and duchess.'

Eventually they played, the piano strong and heavy, the viola quavering, uncertain and sweet. After the very first notes Jude burst into tears again, crying silently and happily over the gay, sentimental piece. The pianist winked, slapped the piano with many flourishes and mock-heroical looks to heaven. The girl stood silent, looking over the throng of dancers. Her excitement had utterly vanished. Except for the bitterness she felt about the wine she was aware only of a dead, miserable boredom in her heart. The party was nothing. The people were strange and foreign to her. The joy had been extinguished in her as the yellow flames had long since been extinguished in the cake, leaving only a cold black wick that she felt would never burn up again.

And then, without warning, she was aware of Masher in the room. Instantly she began trembling. The blood burned and throbbed up through her breast, surging into her throat and head. Why had he come? Who had invited him? The thought of his presence had lurked in the depths of her mind like the secret vague hope of something lovely and impossible. She had wanted him to come with all the agony and joy in her young heart. But she had said nothing. She had not even dared to mention his name. It had given her a sensation of unutterable delight merely to think of his presence there. And now, face to face with him, she was acting foolishly, unable to keep her body still. Her heart fluttered as if she had been frightened. She wanted to shrink away somewhere in an agony of shyness, and remain unseen.

She stood still and watchful during the waltz. He was standing by the table where the birthday-cake, now only a half-circle, had been set aside with the jar of red and white blossoms of may. She was conscious of a vague, insistent ache to be near him, to talk to him, to listen to his voice.

Afterwards, when the waltz had finished and she saw him catch sight of her across the half-empty floor, she tried to act rationally. She gazed at him and smiled. And with that peculiar, swaying, gentle walk, as though he were always afraid of making a sound, he crossed the room and began to talk to her.

'This is a nice way of spending your party, isn't it, staring at your face in the piano?'

She raised her eyes. She felt shy and ashamed before him.

'Forgive me because I didn't ask you to come,' she said.

'Your father asked me, long enough ago.'

'When did you come?'

'When the waltz began.'

'Then you've had no wine?'

'Nothing.'

'Let me fetch you some.'

She slipped away quietly, almost with relief, shy of the pleasure she felt burning up in her. When she returned with the brimming red glasses of wine they sat down behind the piano. He took his glass, lifted it against the naked gaslight.

'What wine is it?'

'Claret,' she said. 'Drink.'

He drank. 'It's a big party,' he remarked.

'I didn't want it,' she flashed.

He felt pained and frustrated. He drained his wine and set the glass on the piano without another word. He did not understand her wild leap from one mood to another. Her first flash of shy, lovely surprise had not been lost on him. He sat pensively, casting long, half-entreating looks at her white neck, her ripening breasts, the dejected fall of her hands in her lap, thrilled in spite of his perplexity by the nearness of her young body, turning even her melancholy into something beautiful.

By and by she moved away to speak to Jude. The pianist never desisted from his dramatic drumming, his lightning gestures. The room was full of whirling dresses, excited conversation, bursts of laughter.

When she returned he was holding a little square parcel in his hand.

'A present for you,' he said simply.

She looked at the parcel quickly and then full into his face with a flash of timid, solemn joy.

'Am I to open it?'

He smiled and she unknotted the string. It was a copy of Thoreau's *Walden*. In amazement she turned the green cover, the pages fluttered, she caught a glimpse, almost as in a dream, of a little wood-cut of a bird.

They were aware for a moment of a curious embarrassment. She was conscious of a queer stupidity arising out of her pleasure. She felt inconceivably touched and delighted. Yet she could say nothing to him. And then he leaned over, pressed back a page of the book and said:

'That's a blue jay.'

They pondered over the book. The picture of the handsome, impudent jay amused them and they were easy again.

'Thank you,' she said. 'Thank you.'

She knew nothing of birds, not so much as the difference between a finch and a sparrow. It was odd that he should have given her such a book. And suddenly she felt a spasm of fear that she would not understand it and that he would come to despise her for this.

They sat and talked to each other. A little later she became suddenly aware of some commotion going on by the door. Alarmed, she went across the room hurriedly, Masher behind her. They pushed through the dancers and passed out of the room and so to the steps leading to the yard below.

Someone was lying at the foot of the stairs and there was a sound of groaning. Masher put his back to the door, cutting off the flood of orange gaslight, the guests and the sound of the piano and the laughter. The girl ran down the steps and peered before her in the dim light. There were two figures and she called, 'Who is it? What has happened?'

She came to the foot of the stairs and she saw her youngest brother bending over another figure. The groaning went on and she caught a smell of sickness.

'What is it? Bill, are you sick, are you sick?' she kept repeating.

'What's the matter?' he said. 'What the hell do you want?'

His voice was thick and she saw him groping about as if he could not see. The odour of sickness grew stronger and presently there was a sound of retching and of the watery sickness spilling itself on the floor and on the lowest steps of the stairs. The stench was foul and putrid and sharp with the added odour of liquor. A young girl in yellow dress was half-lying on the floor, her head propped on a wooden step of the stair. She was very drunk. Her head rolled from side to side like the half-severed head of a rag doll. She was groaning in misery and coughing and spitting the last of the sickness from her mouth.

'Who is it? Who brought her down here?'

'Christ! Interfering! She fell down. I tried to stop her. She fell down I tell you. Now are you satisfied?'

He blundered against her drunkenly, pushed her aside and clasped the girl round the shoulders and struggled to lift her to her feet. 'Stand up!' he muttered. 'For God's sake stand up!' The weight of her body was dead in his hands and the smooth silk of her dress slipped away through his fingers like sand. She fell back heavily, striking her head against the stairs with a groan. He half-fell, thrust his hand in sickness, and swore savagely.

'She's drunk,' he said.

Masher came down the stairs. Pauline was white-faced, with a look of bitter disgust and helplessness. The girl in the yellow dress did not move to let him pass. The air was foul and sickening. Bill waved his arms, exhibiting an unexpected swaggering desire to fight him.

'Take me home,' whispered the girl.

Masher and the boy stood face to face. There was a sombre, lugubrious sneer on the boy's lips. He looked swaggering and flushed and full of conceit, like a young animal.

'Where is her home?' said Masher.

'How should I know! She's married. Let her husband fetch her.'

'Whoever he is he'd smash you! Didn't you bring her here?'

'Yes, I brought her here. What about it, eh? What about it?' he threatened, pushing out his chest.

Masher said nothing and turned away with a gesture of contempt. The boy stood still, mysteriously intimidated. Masher bent down, picked up the girl bodily and carried her into the yard. Her hair fell over her face raggedly and her dress was torn at the bosom, showing her white breast. She groaned and staggered wildly about the yard as if she had landed suddenly after a rush through space. Masher gave one look at her and turned on his heel and went back to Pauline without a word. The girl slowly came to a standstill like a clock-work doll.

He found Pauline leaning against the wall, as if in a trance, half-way up the stairs. To his relief she was not weeping, but her misery had already formed about her like a hard shell, against which his words and entreaties

92

were nothing. They stood in the darkness of the stairs in silence. They could not look at each other.

Presently Pauline begged to be taken outside. At the foot of the stairs there was still the odour of sickness and liquor but the girl and Bill had gone. They crossed the yard and reached the gate of a little paddock at the back of the inn. It was warm and starlight, there was a black horse feeding in the field and there was no sound except the soft swishing noise of the horse grazing.

They stood and talked of what had happened. She told him of the party she had hoped to have, the quarrelling, her hatred of the big, pretentious party where she knew only half the guests.

'Why couldn't it be a quiet party? Why this big affair?' she asked bitterly. 'At home everyone would have seen the cake and the candles. They couldn't help but see it. But it was lost here—no one cared whether the candles were alight or not.'

She told him about the wine.

'It's not that I grudge them the wine—but it's the waste of it, the *waste* of it! Under all this sham and show we haven't a farthing to bless ourselves with—and yet we must have wine. We couldn't do without wine. And all so that my brothers and any fancy woman that they care to bring along could make beasts of themselves!'

She spoke vehemently, beating her hands on the gate with bitter angry blows.

'I'm sick of it all, I'm sick of it all.'

Masher was looking over the field at the horse.

'To-morrow it will seem years away,' he said.

'To-morrow?' she said. 'To-morrow we shall have the second act. They'll lie in bed and be sick again and crawl about like death. That house won't be worth living in!'

For a moment he was silent; and then he was saying suddenly:

93

'Come out into the country with me to-morrow. Let's go out together.'

She was conscious again of a curious fluttering at her heart, as though she had been frightened. He went on: 'We could go and not come back till evening. I could tell you about the birds. It'll be Sunday.'

And suddenly it all seemed inevitable. She must go. Already she could not bear to think of the day if she should not go.

Later she remembered the wood she had seen in the spring.

'I know a beautiful place,' she said.

The following morning, when she walked through the deserted streets to meet him, there was a sense of rest and quietness in her heart. It was very early, the shadows of the houses were still long and dark; in the street she heard the soft, wailing cry of swallows. But the sun was warm and golden and there was a feeling as if summer had come and could never pass away.

She was to meet him outside the town, on a hill beyond the last houses. By a tremendous effort of will she put the memory of the party and the drunkenness behind her. Her brothers had been dead drunk and her father had spent the night on the sofa. She had heard sounds of groaning and retching in the night-time. But she had lost the old vehemence of hatred for them. And the party seemed like some nightmare which she longed desperately to thrust farther and farther away, until she forgot it for ever.

Masher was sitting on a white swing-gate on the road-side, waiting for her. He was plaiting four rushes together, holding the ends in his teeth, like a boy.

'Did you plait your hair this way?' he asked, as they walked on.

'Yes, and I hated it,' she laughed.

'Three strands or four?' he said.

94

'Ask my mother. She did it. I only knew she used to crack my knuckles with the brush when I fidgeted.'

He felt a note of joy in her voice, and there was a sense of jubilant lightness in the way she walked.

They walked on into the high country beyond the town. The land went sweeping away before them with a splendour of distance, the pattern of fields and woods clear and bright in the sharp sunlight to the very edge of the horizon, the infinite summer greenness of it broken by the endless blossoming of hawthorn, like soft gigantic, fluffy knots of whiteness in the nearest fields, then like some faint feather-stitching on the hedges far away. There were fields of buttercups, riotous with bright gold, which they would stay to gaze on in long, amazed silences.

Occasionally they became aware of bean-blossom, over-poweringly fragrant and sweet, as though the field were very near. Masher would climb on a gate and draw long, eager breaths and look over the land. But the field would remain invisible, elusive, and only the scent would creep after them, mysterious, subtle, persistent, as if it would never die away. The corn-fields shone bright emerald in the strong sunlight and the air was gay with the singing of skylarks.

'Look up—can't you see him?—a beauty!'

But the sun would dazzle the girl's eyes and the dancing specks that were the birds would melt into the everlasting blueness of summer sky. When she lowered her eyes again the world would spin before her eyes and the green and gold of the morning would dissolve into a reeling vapour. Feeling faint and drunken and dazzled she would perhaps put out her hand. It would touch the sleeve of Masher's jacket or his hip. Once, when it touched his hand, she withdrew herself hastily. As she did so her fingers brushed quickly over the short soft hairs on the back of his hand. Instantly the tips of her fingers were set tingling and her whole body, as though something electrical had flashed through her, leapt with a shock of joy.

'Where's this you're taking me?' Masher would ask.

It was her secret. He must bear himself in patience. He would see. She would only assure him again and again that it was very beautiful.

They were very simple with one another. She nursed her secret of the wood very closely. And he was never tired of pressing her to give it away.

'Is it Magpie Wood?' he would ask.

She would shake her head.

'But it's *near* to it. I can see by your face. Isn't it, isn't it?'

'No, no!'

'It is! It's Finwick Wood, the place where the four ridings come together. You've been with your father, hunting.'

She would laugh and look secretive and try to change the subject:

'What are the red flowers growing in the spinney?'

'Campions,' he would say indifferently. 'Grannies' nightcaps.'

'They look sleepy and crumpled this morning.'

They would walk on in silence, climbing the white deserted road, going gently upwards in the sunshine.

'It's the fox-covert!' he would burst out.

'Which one?'

'Ah! You're trying to get out of it.'

'I'm sure I never am. You're a bad guesser, that's all.'

'I shall have it yet!'

But soon he would grow tired of guessing. And he would question her with subtle carelessness instead. How big was this place? What sort of trees grew there? Was there a keeper's lodge? When had she first discovered it? They walked steadily on, into the heart of the woodland.

The road mounted, straightened and began to fall gently into another valley. The morning was very still. The shadows of the woods were shortening and folding themselves under the canopy of leaves.

Below lay the wood itself. The girl could see the young oak-trees standing perfectly still against the sky, yellow with late tassels of bloom.

They descended the hill. At the wood the girl stopped and smiled. Her eyes were alight with a rare joy, as though the wood were some strange discovery.

'You never even dreamed it,' she said.

He did not speak. Together they walked into the wood and stood under the oak trees, in the half-golden shadow. He knew the place. Already that spring he had seen the windflowers blowing white in the hollow, the yellow waves of primroses, the pale wild hyacinths running like rippled blue water over the dark earth. He stood staring. Some rabbits cocked their white tails and vanished. It was an old haunt. He knew even where the rabbits went and hid themselves. He felt there was nothing he did not know.

'You don't know it?' she said.

He shook his head. She smiled.

'Shall we go in?' she said.

Even as she spoke she moved off down the path through the wood. He followed her. He said nothing. He saw that she took her joy painfully, intensely, passionately. He saw her look at the young trees, the late clusters of primroses, the patches of red misty campions and lastly at the flood of bluebells ebbing away to the hollow below. She looked very beautiful. Her body was slender and alert in the thin, flowered dress. She took off her hat and ran suddenly with little ecstatic cries to stoop over a bed of oxslips, golden and wide as noon. He noticed the blackness of her hair, the pure whiteness of her slender arms, the soft, tremulous swing of her little breasts under the loose bodice.

Finally they stood still before the bluebells. Beyond the blue hollow the wood straggled away, until the trees stood thinly, revealing broad sunlight. The hyacinths gave out a faint, sweetish smell which mingled with the odour of the dark wood-earth. The girl was breathing quickly.

He let her stare and drink in the sight and scent of the flowers and the flood of sunlight.

And only when she was ready they walked on. She ran on ahead, seeing flowers she did not know, greenish-white candles of blossom thrusting themselves up from the tangle of wild geranium.

She came back to him, holding a flower in her hand. She was breathless and he felt she must exhaust herself.

'What is this?' she said. 'Tell me what it is.'

'It's a white orchis—you see, the flowers are like slippers.'

She breathed the delicate, exotic flower rapturously.

'And look,' he said in a moment, 'Look what this is.'

He was kneeling on the earth, with his hands in the stump of an old ash-tree. She stooped at his side. He seized her hands and thrust her fingers into a hollow in the old bark. She touched a clutch of eggs, warm and hard, like beads.

'What is it?' she whispered.

'A wren's—a jenny's.'

'How did you know? How did you find it?'

'I saw the jenny.'

'When?'

'Come away—she'll forsake,' he urged. 'Come away.'

She went reluctantly at last. She talked of nothing but the nest, the bluebells, the curious orchis-blooms. Masher was quiet. He had already seen the bluebells and the orchis. He had come across the nest a week before. But he

98

must say nothing to her—he must not upset even for one moment the tranquillity of her belief or joy. He could deceive her, but he must not upset for one instant this perfect happiness.

They sat down outside the wood at last. She was exhausted. She lay on her back in the long grass and tried hard to let her body find its peace again in the hot sunshine.

'You're so content,' she said.

She envied suddenly the restful look of his body, the repose of his hands on the grass, his soft stare over the land below. But presently by an effort of will her body relaxed. Her hands lay flat as though in sleep against the buttercup heads in the grass. She continued to feel painfully, foolishly happy. They were together. There was nothing but themselves and the wood and the larks and the yellow field, in a world splashed gold with sunlight.

She lay very still, breathing quietly, the excitement of her heart fluttering down slowly but evenly, like the lark dropping earthwards straight above her face. And with her eyes fixed upon the bird she became unaware of the expression on Masher's face, an expression of half-tortured, half-dreamy watchfulness fixed upon her intently. She felt herself sink away into a state of pure forgetfulness, conscious of nothing but the lark and the sky.

She continued to remain unaware of Masher until he began to kiss her. At the touch of his lips her heart started violently and a warm tumult surged up through her throat and face. She shut her eyes. She felt the heavy, tender pressure of his chest against her breasts and there sprang up a pain of joy in her heart and then a strange physical pain at the mere strength of his embrace about her.

The wood, the air and the field in which they lay seemed to grow suddenly silent. The lark swooped down, settled and ran in the grass. The girl threw her arms about

99

Masher and he in turn thrust his hands into her hair and tangled his fingers in the thick mass of it madly and they clung to each other with passionate desperation, in a blind agony, as though their lips had found suddenly in each other an inexhaustible depth of fresh life and joy.

CHAPTER VII

ONE evening in June Pauline carried the pink-and-white ewer of water upstairs to her bedroom and poured the water slowly into the basin standing in the painted green washing-stand under the window. The air was hot and the sun was still burning fiercely on the roof above her head. Beyond the window the town lay bright and sun-baked, the roofs gleaming a metallic blue in the slanting sunshine, the shadows in the streets below already long with evening. She stood before the window and gazed out, dazed and tired after the factory, her hands pulling her dress over her head with a motion of weariness. She felt as she stretched up her arms and lowered them again to throw the dress over the bed-rail that the strength ran down the veins of her arms and oozed away through her fingers. She had the feeling that she was too weak to shut her hands. She caught an odour of leather and cotton from her body, greasy and sour, and the stale rankness of sweat and the faint stench of the factory.

She remembered the factory with a shudder of her mind and as though to forget it she plunged her hands into the water, letting them rest a long time there. Closing her eyes, however, she saw the place clearly again and felt as if she were sitting there again at the treadle-machine in the topmost room, the sun pouring through the bare slates like fire, the sweat dripping from her forehead in white beads to the machine. The heat of the room, fierce and suffocating, seemed to bear down on her still, and the touch of the water on her hands brought back to her the moment when she had run down to the yard by

101

the engine-shed for a cup of water. She remembered vividly passing the rooms in which the men were working. She had seen them standing over the machines with white faces drenched in sweat, working incessantly as though controlled by the machines. One man had swathed a handkerchief about his forehead like a turban; his face streamed with drops of moisture as if with rain. Another was working without his shirt, his white shoulders gleaming like oil, the black pelt of hair on his chest matted together and soddened with his sweat.

As she stood drinking by the engine-room, a man with black face and arms had rushed up to her to whisper in a desperate voice : 'Give us a drink,' and his lips had moved in time with hers as she drained the cup. When she handed him the cup at last he hurled water over his head and face and drank with piteous greed, cup after cup, drowning his breath to great desperate gasps, looking as though ready to die as he lolled back, limp, white and defeated, against the wall.

She lingered over the pleasure of her own washing, soaping her shoulders and her breasts until a flush of pink stole over her skin. The sweetness of her cleaned body, the scent of soap making her shoulders and her bosom fragrant once more, filled her slowly with fresh life. Presently when she had thrown off her damp, sour clothes and had slipped on a fresh skirt, she bathed her feet, existing in a world of quietness, relaxing blissfully, the suspense of the day gone, every breath a profound relief.

Later, as she lay on the bed in her skirt and turned over the pages of a book that Masher had lent her, she heard desultory scraps of conversation from the yards below and the sound of her father whistling the dogs as he prepared to go off for the evening somewhere.

'Warmish,' she heard him say.

'Christ!' called a woman, 'I've lost a stone since dinner.'

'You'll fatten up again!' he called back to her.

'I like your lousy cheek,' she bawled.

'Have a drink?' he teased her.

'You ain't got no bloody drink but what you want it yourself!' she cried.

She heard him laugh derisively at the end of the yard and his last whistle to the dogs, and the murmur of conversation beneath the window went on again.

When twilight began to fall and she too went down to sit where the shadows were heavy and cooler, women were still grouped in the narrow yard between the houses. They were sitting on chairs and boxes, bantering and gossiping and eating cheese and spring-onions between white thicknesses of bread. Fanny and her mother were also there, Fanny with her new-born child.

'That'll be the day,' said a woman to Fanny, 'when that little joker'll sit up and ask for a spring-onion.'

'Never mind onions! You thank Christ,' said the woman Emma, who had shouted at Quintus, 'he ain't a gal. Gals are a trouble morning and night, all their damned lives. I took my stays off at eleven o'clock this morning and they ain't dry yet. That's being a gal.'

Fanny, very pale, sitting in a rocking-chair drawn up over the threshold, held her child solemnly and quietly, and as if entreating the women to talk in lower tones, murmured:

'He's asleep now,' and lowered her sallow face over the child's white head, as though to protect it from the faintest sound. The child lay still at her breast, white and immobile, and presently the painter's wife, a large woman with strong red arms which she held constantly folded over her breast, made a gesture as though to take it from her:

'Now that I've finished my morsel o' supper,' she said, 'let me take him a minute and you rest yourself.'

'He's asleep now,' said the girl. A look of stubbornness and pride came over her face, as if in protection of the child.

'You'll wear your bones clean down to nothing, and waste away like a tallow candle.'

'I ain't tired,' said the girl. 'He's so light I don't know I've got him.'

She parted her lips in a smile of mild superiority and shook her head.

'I feel like a bit o' damn candle myself,' sighed the woman Quintus had teased.

Pauline sat down on the step of the house and rested her head against the arm of the rocking-chair and the chair swung to and fro like the branch of a tree in a soft wind. The women sat about her, fanning their faces or munching their bread and there was an effect of languid motion in the yard, though the air itself seemed to hang between the houses without tremor or life.

Thinking of nothing but the weariness of her body and gazing dreamily at the white face of the child, perfectly serene and oblivious at the breast of his mother, she felt hardly conscious of what went on about her. Presently however she smiled at the voice of Emma calling:

'Adam, my flower, be a blessed angel and fetch my stays for me.'

The girl, looking up, saw the boy go sheepishly forward and stand among the women, serious and ill-at-ease at their laughter.

'That's right, my pigeon, Emma knew what a boy you were. They hang on the line in my yard, my angel. If they're dry now, you bring 'em here.'

'Let me go,' said a woman. 'He wouldn't know a pair of stays if he saw one.'

'Come here, Adam my daisy. You know what a pair of stays are, don't you?'

'Yes.'

'Christ, I should think he knows a pair of stays at his time of life. On the line in my yard, my angel, off you go!'

The boy moved off slowly, as if wondering, and the painter sitting on the doorstep of his house, called after him:

'They're pink, my thon.'

'Here!' blazed Emma, 'who the hell told you they were pink, inquisitive?'

'Didn't I thee 'em on the line when I came by? That'th who told me.'

'Oh! mind your business!' she flashed back. 'Eat your onion!'

A young woman standing against a water-butt, her figure showing the faint curve of pregnancy, spoke suddenly whilst eating:

'I done nothing but eat onions ever since I came and stood here.'

'My old man grew them onions,' said Emma. 'There's strength in 'em.'

'I feel just as if I could go on eating onions till doom. Onions and nothing else but onions.'

An older woman, with hair already grey above her yellowish temples, said in a low voice:

'I recollect I did nothing else but want to gather white violets. All the time I wanted to be picking violets and allus white ones. That's how I was.'

'I never had no time to think of violets,' said Emma.

'Well, that's how I was.'

'My old man had the blues three days running and led me dance enough, without violets.'

The boy appeared in the yard with the stays, holding them awkwardly before him in both hands, so that the pink laces dangled about his knees.

At the sight of him the women laughed and he blushed

deeply and gave the stays into Emma's hands hastily. She seized the stays and made extravagant gestures and folded the corsets about her waist, but over her skirt the buckles would not meet each other and she suddenly flung the corsets over her head and danced in heavy mimicry of a ballet-dancer, kicking out her fat legs and flinging back her coarse face, mocking some classical pose of cold, disdainful beauty. The women broke into half-hysterical laughter, their voices like excited hens', their heads shaking with helpless gaiety. The painter, sitting on the doorstep with his head between knees, coughed and spat like a man in pain. His wife hammered his back with great blows of her flat red hands. Against the water-barrel, near which the boy was standing, sheepishly smiling, the pregnant girl hastily threw away the green stalk of an onion and laughed softly with almost inward laughter, until the tears swelled into her eyes and ran down her smiling face. A little white terrier dashed hither and thither among the chairs, barking shrilly, and lower down the row of houses a woman with a beautiful pigtail of untidy black hair thrust her head from a bedroom window, shouting as shrilly as the dog barked to know what had happened.

'I've winded myself, that's what's happened. Christ! I feel like a churn of milk on the turn in a thunderstorm. It's a sign I can't dance like I did.'

Emma threw herself back into the chair again. Closing her eyes with an expression of elegance and shaping her corsets like a fan, she proceeded to fan her crimson face languidly, looking like a dowager, and the laughter about her broke out afresh again.

During all this, sitting in the rocking-chair with her face low down over the face of the child, Fanny remained statuesque and dreamy, as though oblivious as the child itself of the excitement and laughter.

The child was wrapped in a black shawl, and the boy,

from his place by the water-butt, could see nothing but a black shape lying in the white embrace of the girl's long arms. The face of the girl herself he could see clearly, however, and while Emma cooled herself with the pink fan of her corsets, he felt himself arrested by its expression of beautiful, pure content. He saw this contentment also in her long stares at the child's face and the endearing movements of her white hands.

He had become accustomed to the utter stillness of all this when suddenly she raised the child bodily and took it from the crook of one arm to the other. She lifted the child gently and delicately, but a tassel from the shawl dropped over its face. As she brushed the tassel away her fingers by accident touched the child's forehead and she drew them away hastily, with a gesture of self-reproach, afraid of waking him.

The boy saw the white face lying in perfect repose. He heard Emma, who had dropped her stays and let her arms fall strengthlessly into her lap, breathe out:

'Jesus! I'm sure my heart'll stop beating.'

The woman with the beautiful long pigtail came into the yard, twining the ends of black hair about her finger, but the boy did not glance at her.

He was watching instead the girl's hand as it approached the face of the child again. He saw the hand withdraw itself very slowly and he saw a curious expression come to birth in her eyes, an expression at first of puzzled unrest, then of doubt, and finally of fear itself. The chatter and laughter about him went on, but it grew confused and he was conscious of nothing but the deathly fear in Fanny's face. Sitting perfectly immobile, her face like white stone, utterly rigid except for the wild, quick eyes alternately raising themselves to the women and lowering to the child again, she struck a kind of horror into his heart, and when he saw her hands begin to flutter up and down the

107

shawl, rapidly and tremulously, as if with signals of distress, he felt hypnotized, conscious of nothing but her unhappy terror.

The girl leaning against the water-butt beside him straightened herself up and spoke:

'I'll go off my head if I don't eat another onion,' she said.

She began to walk slowly away. The boy stood motionless. He saw a moment later the dumb, stony expression on Fanny's face broken; the lips quivered; the head began to dart this way and that, like a frightened bird's.

Suddenly he caught distinctly the words, 'Mother, mother,' repeated in a whisper, 'Mother!' He saw the girl stagger to her feet, looking wildly at the women, and he was conscious suddenly of a strange confusion in the yard and of the women running in all directions. He saw Pauline standing silent and tense by the rocking-chair and he noticed the pink stays lying in the chair where Emma had left them. He heard the low, plaintive voice of Emma repeating, 'God love us!' making a sudden silence. Next moment the child was in the arms of the painter's wife and Fanny was shrieking and waving her arms in a fury of madness that seemed to chill his blood and draw the sweat from his brow like a freezing dew.

'That baby's dead,' he heard a whisper. 'I felt of its fingers and they were like ice. I know it's dead.'

'You bet ith a gonner, poor kid!' said the painter aloud.

'Will you keep your damn mouth shut?' came a whisper.

A little knot of women obscured the Harpers' doorway. Jarred by the elbow of the woman with the pigtail, the rocking-chair was set in motion again and began swaying to and fro slowly and solemnly, like the pendulum of an old clock. An altercation of furious whispers arose between the painter and his wife and the painter was driven away with threats of blows.

The pregnant girl began to walk out of the yard with difficulty; her face was deathly and she stumbled weakly and sat heavily in the chair where the pink stays lay. A woman without a blouse came running up from nowhere.

The painter's wife, fat, serious and capable, came out of the house, stood on the doorstep and crooked her finger threateningly.

'Surely to God you can do something besides stand there like a dummy? Fetch the doctor!'

A series of wild, piteous shrieks came from within the house. The painter was turning away when he was urged by a furious commanding whisper:

'By God, I'll wring your neck if you don't shift yourself.'

The boy stood utterly still. His body had broken into a sweat of sickly terror.

A moment later Pauline suddenly appeared from the house and came to him.

'Run to *The Angel* and fetch my father,' she said.

He gazed at her and hesitated. At the back of his mind he felt there lay something he wished to say to her. During a brief silence she looked at him with an unflickering earnest gaze. They were alone in the yard except for the girl sitting in the chair with her head on her breast, trembling and oblivious of them.

Suddenly, suspecting his hesitation to mean unwillingness or fear, Pauline declared in a low voice:

'I'll come with you.'

As he went with her along by the row of houses and through the street to the heart of the town his mind was never free of the white images of Fanny's face watching the face of her child. He recalled also the wild shriek the girl had given and often he shut his eyes against the memory of her madly-waving arms. All his thoughts were chaotic and his mind was filled with vague miseries. His acquaintance with death had been brief. But the realization of death had fixed itself within him and he bore it without illusions, regarding it with a gigantic, steadfast fear.

During all that journey, as they hurried hither and thither to find Quintus, he did not once speak to the girl and she in her turn never opened her lips to him. He often looked up at her, but she hardly ever acknowledged him and he constantly wondered why she ignored him, what she was thinking, and why she hurried on as though she were running away.

After the child's death he dared not go into the house for a long time. When finally he did return he could not rid himself of the notion that the body lay hidden in the black oak box, covered with the green cloth blazing with the golden harp.

CHAPTER VIII

THE stream came languidly down through flat meadows, turning with long shallow bends, flowing almost to stillness in dark pools lying without sunlight under arches of haw-thorn and elder-trees, escaping again to narrow reaches of white stones and sand where the water flashed swiftly, without depth. The banks were steep and between the tufts of tall grass the earth was soft and reddish, like dark sand. Here and there willow-trees strained out over the water and in the moist places there were late forget-me-nots that had not lost their delicacy and forests of willow-herb flecked with pink bloom.

Adam had chosen a group of trees under which to sit. The shadows were cool under the trees and Pauline was lying on her side in the grass. She was dressed in a thin white summer frock and she was lazily throwing pieces of bread to the water. Adam was a little distance away, un-ravelling his tackle, and Masher was choosing a worm to put on the hook for him. Troops of very tiny fish were already arriving to feed on the bread.

The sight of the fish excited the boy and the instinct for quietness left him. As soon as the worm was hooked he seized the rod and cast the line, but the hook became caught in the outward branches of a willow-tree. Adam and Masher grew very hot untangling the line and it was a long time before the red float sat securely on the water.

When the float was at rest and the boy sat as if entranced while watching it, Masher sat down by Pauline in the grass. They sat drinking in the warmth of the after-noon, the soft summer murmurs about them and the heavy

111

scent of ripening grass, not moving or speaking. Bees began to work in the willow-herb with low murmurs and a writing-lark kept up its song sweetly but monotonously close at hand. Pauline turned over on her back and looked at the sky through leaves.

'What tree is this?' she said at last.

'It's an ash,' he told her.

'How do you know it's an ash?'

'I know by the leaves,' he said. 'They branch out in pairs from one long stem.'

'Supposing it was winter,' she said, 'and there were no leaves? Would you know it then?'

'I'd know by the way the branches dip at the end and curve up again.'

'Do they always dip and curve up again?'

'Not always. Sometimes they don't weep at all.'

'How would you know then?' she said.

'I'd know by the black buds or the feathery flowers or the bark or the locks-and-keys. Something would tell me.'

'Do you know other trees too?'

'Most trees,' he said.

'How is it you know and I don't know? I could live under a tree all my life and not know what it was.'

'I seem to have known all my life which was an ash,' he said, 'and which was an elm and all the rest. You forget what you learn sometimes but you don't forget the things you were born with.'

She sat up and looked round and said:

'What are the other trees you can see from here?'

They sat closer to each other and one by one he pointed out to her the trees as far as the eye could reach, speaking softly for the sake of the boy, telling her which were the elms and oaks, and lingering a little over the beeches and poplars. In one corner of the field where they were sitting stood a solitary larch, bright emerald against the sky. 'It's

like a Christmas-tree,' she said. They let their eyes remain
on it for a long time, until she knew it familiarly. 'You'd
know a larch again if you lived to be a hundred,' he said.
The fresh knowledge of the trees stimulated her and she
had implicit faith in all he told her. It seemed to her very
wonderful that he should know so much, and at times she
followed the way of his finger half-worshipfully.

There were no fish biting and presently Masher went
and sat on the bank beside the boy. Tiddlers had eaten
the bread and were clustered about his float, attacking it
greedily. There were no other fish to be seen and the worm
hung pink and dead in the water.

'A fish came out and looked at the worm and went
away,' said the boy.

'Very big?'

'Very big!'

The little fish became a great nuisance and at last
Masher took out the line and opened the tobacco-tin and
hooked on another worm. Again the boy cast in and again
they sat in silence on the bank, watching and waiting. The
afternoon unfurled itself like a soft flower and the float lay
motionless, the sun filtering in golden and fretted shapes
through the leaves, striking through the pool with a serene
light, leaving the water as clear and bright as yellow wine.
The girl lay on her back again, looking at the sky. By and
by a fish came swiftly out of the shadows, but it struck
away, ignoring the worm, and only the boy caught a
glimpse of it passing into the reeds. The tiny fish came
and attacked the float again. A little larger fish appeared,
circled about the hook and as if in contempt struck
languidly away.

'They're not feeding,' said Masher. 'We should have
brought a little bran and mixed it with mud and thrown
that in. That's a sort of physic for them and they feed
like wolves after it. I could have brought the bran.'

'Couldn't we try them with bread?'

'You get the tiddlers if you try with bread.'

'Is dough good bait?'

'Dough's not bad. But a roach will take cheese sometimes, or a maggot, and a handful of boiled wheat's as good as anything.'

'Can you eat roach?'

'Eat them?'

'Yes.'

'They melt in your mouth like butter! But you ought to be in deeper water—up there, past that willow. It's three or four feet there.'

The boy took his line beyond the willow-tree and Masher lay back and leaned his head against the trunk of the tree. Sleepily and with a half-smile, in a voice the boy could not hear, he turned to Pauline and said:

'It's too bright for fish. He won't catch anything.'

Instantly, in a tone of mingled reproof and entreaty which took him by surprise, she answered:

'Don't laugh at the boy.'

'Laugh?' he said.

'His head has been full of dreams of the fish he has caught.'

'I didn't think of laughing.'

'You didn't think—and yet you did laugh. You did. You smiled. I saw you. And if the boy had seen it too he'd have been unhappy.'

She had never before expressed even the faintest reproach of anything he had done or said. He looked at her suddenly with a frown; the dark, puzzled shadow of which she was sometimes afraid made its appearance like a tight, complex knot between his brows. As though hardly conscious of him she continued to stare at the water, her face solemn and pale, like a mask. And he said:

'You aren't unhappy, are you?'

She turned her head with a start, as if he had frightened her. The single word 'Unhappy?' which she spoke very slowly, was heavy with surprise. He felt her gaze fix itself at once upon his brows. He lifted them and then drew them down again, disquieted by her long, solemn look at them. Suddenly she shook her head, quite violently, her eyes at the same time round and wonder-struck, her expression half-smiling, though not amused.

It was as if he had disturbed her from some momentary dream; and she asked suddenly:

'Why did you ask that?'

'Because you spoke about the boy. It was natural to ask,' he answered. 'You're not always happy with me?'

To his astonishment she looked at him quickly, as though she too were surprised, and said:

'Of course I am!' And then, as if as an afterthought: 'I begin to look for it now.'

She spoke with perfect simplicity, in a tone almost as if she were confessing something a little reluctantly. For a moment he reflected and then said:

'Now? But you haven't always been happy with me?'

'Always,' she answered immediately. 'Since the very beginning.'

'Since the beginning?'

'Yes,' she said. The word was spoken with perfect conviction. He smiled involuntarily, and she added at once:

'But now I begin to look into the future a little more.'

He did not know what to think, still less what to say in answer to this, and he merely let the smile linger vaguely on his lips. She was looking at him intently, as though anxious to see how he accepted her words, and she broke out at once:

'And now you're laughing at me!'

'Never!'

'You think it's foolish.'

115

'I don't,' he declared. 'But I've given up contemplating the future.'

For the first time she refused to meet his gaze. She looked suddenly away into the green precipices and flags of weed waving solemnly under the water.

'The future is all right—it's splendid—but it will take care of itself,' he went on. 'That's all I care. The present—now—this afternoon—this moment, that's what matters if you like.'

'Nothing else?' she said.

'The past as well if you like. We build on that.'

'But not the future?' she asked.

'For all you know there may be no future,' he said.

Her gaze, returning quickly back from its contemplation of the dark, still water, fixed itself upon him with wide, painful astonishment. They were both silent; and then the pain in her glance resolved itself into something different, something by which she plainly meant both to pity and censure him. And slowly she observed:

'There's the difference between us.'

He reflected on the words.

'But you seem to be obsessed with the future,' he said after a moment.

'Obsessed?'

'It seems to be everything to you.'

She spoke in a voice of passionate surprise, almost angrily:

'Of course it's everything. What else could it be?'

He did not answer, and his brow lowered itself again.

'What else could it be?' she repeated. 'What did you think it could be? You don't expect me to think of the present in this place, do you? Not among that lot, living on tick, and all that?'

'I don't know,' he said uncertainly.

'But you don't think I want to go on living there?'

'I don't know what I thought,' he said.

'But I hate it, I've always hated it!' she exclaimed. 'I hate it, I tell you!'

He looked about him sharply, a little confused, and then said to her:

'The boy will hear.'

She looked at him wildly, with an expression of desperate entreaty, as if at a loss for a reply. And then suddenly she lowered her head and a torrent of quiet, excited words began to run from her lips. He looked at her astounded. 'I used to cry myself to sleep,' he heard her say. 'And on the days when I never saw you I often made myself ill—that's silly, but I felt sick, I tell you. I felt if I could have seen you—you understand, don't you?—if I could have been with you a moment, that would have meant everything. And now I've told you. It sounds silly, but you understand, don't you? You understand? I haven't told you before—I felt you'd understand without that. And I'm so sick when I think of it again. Oh! God I'm so sick of it.'

She had spoken all the time without looking at him, in a voice of hurried insistence, but very quietly. Embarrassed, and in turn touched and puzzled by her words, he turned his head to see the boy standing behind him, holding the fishing-rod in his hands, waiting for him to come.

'Come and fish in another pool,' said the boy.

'In a moment,' he said.

'The boy wants to go farther up-stream for a bit,' he said to the girl.

Sitting perfectly still, she was gazing once again at the dark water, and she did not move or speak in reply, as if she were content to be oblivious of him.

A little relieved, he turned away with the boy and they

117

walked slowly away up-stream, looking for fresh pools in which to fish, stopping now and then to peer into the darker places. It was very hot in the meadow: over everything lay a still blaze of sunshine; the grey willow-leaves flagged in the bright light and there was not a breath of wind. They presently came to a pool that was shallower than the last, and Masher, kneeling down on the bank and leaning over, saw a sleepy gudgeon lying beside a stone. The water was flooded with yellow light and the worm seemed almost white as it sank away.

The worm dangled before the gudgeon's nose and attracted its attention, but Masher drew the worm gently away, enticing the fish to follow, and the boy held his breath. In a moment the fish made a stirring motion, shot forward and regarded the worm from closer quarters. The pool, the air, the whole world seemed suddenly to remain very still, as if holding its breath too, and then the gudgeon seemed to quiver, its mouth touching the worm, and slowly, in a profound suspense, the worm began to disappear. The boy felt a choking sensation in his throat, anxious to cry out, but Masher never moved and the gudgeon lay still also. Slowly the worm vanished and suddenly the gudgeon started, wild and trapped, the hook in its throat, and with a flick of his hand Masher jerked it high out of the pool, its greyish body flashing in the sunshine, sprinkling beads of water that fell like diamonds and were spirited away.

The gudgeon seemed very small when the hook was taken from its throat and it lay gasping in the grass. There was a sense of disappointment in the boy's heart suddenly. The fish itself was unimportant and all the wonder and excitement that lay in deluding and catching it had gone. On the grass it was a poor, pitiful thing, worthy of contempt; in the water it had seemed large and beautiful, exciting and alluring him with its sleepy loveliness. Now he saw only its contemptible length, and its gasping, ugly gills and he was willing for Masher to throw it back again.

The gudgeon sank away into the shadows, and Masher prepared another worm.

They fished again and gradually the boy's desire was rekindled again. He sat absorbed and presently Masher left him and walked along the stream to where he had left Pauline. The sun was like fire on his bare head and he could see the heat trembling in the distance over the bare line of a higher field.

He walked slowly; his feet were noiseless in the grass and he was standing over the girl before she was aware. Her heart gave a violent start and she uttered a little cry:

'You frightened me.'

'Adam is fishing for gudgeon in another pool,' he said.

He sat down by her, leaning back on his elbow. She sat as he had left her, staring at the pool.

'I meant to ask you something,' she said, after a moment's silence.

'Yes?' he said, and he was conscious of his heart beating with strange rapidity.

There was a moment of silence, and then, as if seeking deliberately to make him forget where their conversation had broken off, she said:

'Which tree is it that grows up tall and straight, like a church spire?'

'A poplar,' he said.

'It's a beautiful tree, that one,' she said.

'We used to see them in France a good deal,' he told her. 'I think it's a southern tree. They used to go on mile after mile and we got tired of them after seeing them a bit. They're not friendly, like English trees.'

'And then that flower, the pink flower, which grows all along the brook. I'd like to know what that is.'

'Willow-herb,' he said.

'Did you see that in France too?' she asked.

He shook his head.

'I can't remember.'

A sudden puff of breeze shook the ash-tree overhead and then the air became motionless again.

'What were you in France? What did you do?' she said.

'I was a stretcher-bearer.'

She was silent.

'Why talk about it?' he said. He looked faintly resentful.

'I was a child at the time,' she said. 'I don't know anything.'

Again they were silent, but again an eager curiosity possessed her, an overpowering need to talk with him.

'I remember the soldiers,' she said. 'We had soldiers put on us, three at one time and four at another. God alone knows how we used to sleep.'

'But you were very excited?'

'Yes, I was excited. I used to brush their tunics and clean their badges for them.'

'We weren't very excited,' he said.

They sat quietly for a little time, pondering. There was not a cloud in the sky.

'The war made me fat,' he said. 'I had a face like a dumpling.'

'You've changed since then.'

'Yes,' he said.

She moved her position and half-reclined on the earth.

'I saw a man once,' he went on, speaking in a detached voice, almost as if she were not there, 'who had been gassed. He came into the dug-out where I was sitting with some Irish Fusiliers. He looked very white and he walked just as though he was drunk. He reeled everywhere. We didn't know what to do, and then after a moment or two he fell on the ground and began to kick and squirm and then we knew there was no need to do anything. He was past our help, and we looked at it like this. If we helped him perhaps he would live a little longer, perhaps ten minutes or even half an hour, but not much longer. And what's half an hour? He was in agony and if we let him die it was merciful. That was best. And so we stood and sat to watch him die. He was an Irishman too, and every minute he would keep saying "Mother of God, won't somebody help me? Holy Virgin, dear blessed Mother of God, won't somebody help me? Won't somebody do anything for me?" And so he kept on. "Holy Mary, make them do something to help me." And then he turned yellow, a queer yellow, almost green, and he didn't cry quite so much and we knew he would die quickly. And then in a moment he said "Dear Blessed Mother of God, have mercy on me!" And then he tried to say it again but the rattle had begun and his face had turned quite green. When he died we were relieved. I remember I felt almost happy. But I see it a little differently now.'

By degrees the tone of detachment had passed out of his voice, and had become replaced by emotion, and on his face was an expression the girl had never seen there before, soft, almost mystical, profoundly suffering. She had listened intently, and the happening rose up vividly before her eyes and she was allied by a new, secret contact to him.

Suddenly, as if to communicate what she felt, she said:

'There will be a time when you have forgotten all that!'

'I shan't forget,' he said.

'But there are some things you do forget,' she said.

'For a little while you seem to forget, certainly, but more often a thing keeps with you, like your shadow. You forget it for years and then suddenly you know it's there again.'

He was winding a piece of grass, spiral-fashion, about his finger, not looking at her.

'The war changed your life,' she said.

'If you like. I got fatter in the face and I was wounded in the right foot.'

He smiled and went on:

'I've gone thin again but I still feel the wound.'

'And that's what made you a socialist?' she said.

'I was a socialist already,' he said. 'I used to wave banners and I learnt boxing to protect myself. Nice days. I thought I should like to burn the house of every rich man in the country and make them live in three rooms and a kitchen on ten shillings a week. But I got tired of it. I read a bit of philosophy and thought a little more and it struck me that if you hurt a man's house or took his wealth away it was no good if you left him his brain and his spirit. It's hard to rob a man of what he's born with. And then I read Thoreau—the book called *Walden*—you remember?'

'Yes, I have read it all.'

'And I knew at once that if I could choose the life I was to live, it would be a life like that.'

'You would give up everything?'

'Everything.'

'Just as Thoreau did?'

'Yes.'

'And what about friends, and companionship?' she asked.

'I should be free to do what I wished.'

'Quite free?'

'Yes, absolutely free. No man ought to be chained.'

'You'd go away?'

'Yes,' he said. 'Perhaps I should go away.'

At the words she lifted up her face to him, sharply and eagerly, as if they had been the words she wanted to hear.

122

But a moment later she heard him go on speaking in a sceptical, bitter voice:

'That's what I like to think, anyhow. I like to think that. I've always liked to think about the fresh start and the simple life and so on. It's a good dream. You live in a place and life is rotten and you keep thinking: "If only I could live somewhere different, life would be wonderful." That's what you think. But when you move away life is just the same—what you make it. No man can alter that.'

She turned away her head and buried her face in the grass. The grass was like a forest of brilliant green hung with creepers and blossoms and pink cranesbill and white clover bloom. The scent of the flowers and the grass was strong and ripe and the seed-heads were dusty and heavy, and there was an odour of earth. She closed her eyes. She could not look at him or listen any longer. She hated these bitter and insufferable words.

But suddenly she was conscious of a shadow moving across her face and of something bearing tenderly down upon her breast. A button on Masher's jacket began to press on her bosom. It pained her but she endured it without moving. And presently she heard his voice in a tender reassuring whisper: 'Don't be unhappy. It may happen. It will happen. Don't be unhappy.' And slowly he began to kiss her, and as the kiss was prolonged she felt as if she were falling into space, and she clung wildly to his shoulders.

When the kiss had ended Masher raised his face and gazed at her. He saw her face once again like a mask; the lids of her eyes were faintly blue and her face was tinged with pink at the cheek-bones, as if two fingers had been pressed there. She was disquietingly beautiful, but at the back of his mind lay a faint suspicion of guilt, as if he had deceived her.

They continued to lie there kissing and touching each other. The clover was very sweet and the heat did not lessen and the cloud of flies dancing above them would not go away. At intervals they attempted a conversation, but the words lost their sequence and became murmurings of entreaty, very tender. She opened her eyes, smiled slowly, and shut them again, and he ran his hands with half-plaintive murmurs across her breast.

Later they heard the boy's cry in the deep stillness of the afternoon. They sat upright and saw him running towards them, carrying something in his hand. He waved his hand, displaying a roach he had caught; suddenly it wriggled from his hand and fell in the grass and he dropped on his knees to capture it again. Presently he scrambled on and came up to them, his eyes flashing like beads and his words running into each other. He knelt down and put the fish on the grass for Pauline and Masher to see; it was a splendid roach, dying as it wriggled and jumped in the hot sun. Masher went to the brook and cut a handful of broad reeds, and very carefully he and the boy laid the roach in them, knotting the ends of the reeds to make a kind of basket. Then they wrapped a handkerchief about the reeds and the boy sprinkled the whole with water, running to and from the brook with wild cries, urging Masher to come and fish again.

Presently Masher went back to the pool with the boy. The sun had veered to the west and the light was pouring hot and golden under the drooping leaves of the tree. Pauline lay back and stared in thought at the tree and the sky. And slowly she became conscious that she had lost the ecstasy brought about by the kiss he had given her. There had been a time when the joy of his presence would remain with her for days, but it was different now.

Deep in her heart she felt for a moment or two uncertain of him. She felt afraid of his bitterness and his mood of cynical recollection. She was no longer perfectly sure of him. She felt vaguely that somewhere between them there must exist a fundamental difference, a rift, a weakness in the things which held them together. If that were so, what would happen? she asked herself. Where would be the end of it all? What if he should fail her, throw up everything and do as he had always longed to do? There was a sudden cold emptiness in her heart. And for a moment she half-hated him, despising his bitterness and all the things which she felt might take him away from her. But the moment passed. And suddenly she was conscious of a flood of tenderness for him. She still had a sublime faith in him. She still trusted him infinitely. He had changed her life. He had revolutionized her thoughts and her beliefs and her ideals. He had smashed down her religion and had made her believe in a vague, visionary, splendid state on earth when things would be better. Because of him she had grown, had changed, had begun to feel life. She had come no longer to believe in God. She believed in Masher. Nothing could shatter the foundation of her faith in him. Nothing could make her change or falter in the belief that in spite of everything he would take her away. She knew that it would happen, that it must happen. The old virgin, child-like state of her mind, with its vague desires, its ideals and dreamy longings, had vanished utterly, and in its place had sprung up this clear, burning, passionate purpose, without illusions, miraculously big in her life like a child in the womb, bringing with it a flood of rapturous, hopeless love and the knowledge and determination that she could not rest until she had been delivered.

CHAPTER IX

ONE evening late in August Masher was sitting in the kitchen behind the shop, slowly eating a kipper he had cooked for himself at the gas-ring standing by the sink in the corner. The dirty frying-pan and a few unwashed dishes lay in the sink and the air was rank with the smell of fish. He was drinking a cup of strong tea with the kipper; the cup had no handle, the saucer did not match and he held the broken cup with difficulty, bringing it to his lips like a bowl. On the table there was a loaf of bread, some butter and a pot of pepper. The table-cloth was dirty, ringed with tea-stains and blotched with dark patches of grease. Besides the chair in which he was sitting there was an American leather arm-chair, torn on the left arm, and another chair with a broken back. A sewing-machine stood in another corner. On the sewing-machine stood some books and a tinsel rose-bowl half full of blown pink roses. The room, washed in a violent shade of blue with the walls darkened by stains of grease, had a sordid look. The window looked out on a dirty narrow yard bounded by a tarred wooden fence, beyond which houses rose up in close succession, without end. There was a dog-kennel in the yard and beside it a rough rust-coloured mongrel lying asleep on a chain. Against the fence was a solitary patch of earth; a cluster of sunflowers had reached the height of the fence and a single yellow flower had opened and stood with its face to the west, in the evening sun.

Sarah Jonathan came in from the shop at intervals

while Masher was eating. She was dressed in a slovenly fashion, wearing a loose faded red pinafore and soft carpet-slippers. Her gait was quick and sharp and she shuffled her slippered feet as she walked. She would come in without a word, take down a little red book, write in the credits and go out quickly again. Going out, she would look at Masher. There was something in her glance covert but critical, a flash of something guardedly hostile, and her head would move sharply in contempt. She would sometimes look at him more fixedly and for longer intervals, her eyes hard and the look very penetrative, as if she half-wished to attract his attention.

Masher picked up a newspaper and propped it against the tea-pot and began reading. He read the political news and the references to books. Someone came into the shop to have his snuff-box filled and half-consciously Masher listened to the strong snorts that followed and the money clinking across the counter. A child entered for a pint of vinegar, and he heard the squeak of the wooden tap under the counter. The child did not pay, and as Sarah was about to enter the credit a woman came in for some tea. He heard them holding a conversation about a funeral. The woman did not pay for the tea.

Sarah came into the kitchen again and wrote in the credit book the details of the tea and the vinegar.

'Things are rotten,' she said. 'Foresters ain't paid for six weeks.'

Masher picked up the newspaper, folded it and propped it against the tea-pot again.

'They live on tick,' he said. 'You must live on tick, that's all.'

'I'm an honest woman,' she burst out. 'Not so much of your living on tick.'

'It's tick that makes the clock go round.'

'I've lived for forty years and paid for what I've had

127

without tick; I wouldn't sleep at nights if I didn't pay for what I had.'

'Cut me some bread, will you?'

She seized the knife and pressed the loaf against her bosom and cut viciously.

'And what's more, I couldn't live as some folks do. I'd rather die. Food never paid for and clothes from one pack-man and another and the whole going-on a sham.'

'When there's no wind the ship won't sail.'

'There's wind in this case.'

He spread a little butter on the slice of bread and looked up.

'In Foresters?'

'You know it ain't Foresters,' she said.

'I know it ain't Foresters? How's that?'

'You know it couldn't be Foresters. The old man's thrown out, and Polly on a water-bed, and Chrissie on half-time. That's a lot, ain't it?'

'Well, who is it?'

'If you don't know,' she flashed, 'I'm damned if I ever tell you.'

'I don't want to know.'

'You will know.'

She spoke with significance, very quietly, and with an air of half-bitter certainty. A spasm of surprise went through him swiftly, sharpening to the conviction that she was talking about the Harpers and that she knew of Pauline. The conviction seemed to strike in him a spark of anger and the anger gave him a kind of inexorable pleasure and he involuntarily raised his eyes and looked at her.

'Well?'

'I've put up with your socialism and your fine ideas for a long time, but now it comes to a chip of a girl I don't put up with that!'

128

He lowered his eyes and said:

'This kipper was salt.'

'You hear what I say?'

'I'm listening.'

'I don't put up with that chip of a girl!'

'What girl?'

'You don't take me in! You know what girl.'

'She's a beautiful girl,' he said.

'If she's so beautiful, take her!' she sneered. 'See? Take her and live on tick with her for what she'll give you. It don't matter to me, see? It don't matter. I shall have the shop.'

'By God! Haven't you always had the damned shop!'

They glared at each other, but there were sudden footsteps in the shop and Sarah hastily left the kitchen. Masher heard voices and the chink of money. He lifted his cup and drank the remainder of his tea. He was shaking all over, he felt full of a sickening anger, his brain was tormented by the thought of the girl and the hatred he felt for Sarah. He suddenly wanted to act with decisive deliberation, expressing his intention about the girl clearly, his soul shrinking from an alternative of increasing pettiness and spite. He would have been glad of one moment of logical thought, but his reason seemed numb and his finer self subdued; his thoughts crowded upon each other with madness and he was conscious of an instinct for malice and cruelty, a primitive need to express himself violently.

He heard Sarah returning, and the need conquered him. He sprang to his feet and half-shouted 'So I'm to go with her?' and tore down his jacket from the peg behind the door and struggled into it madly. The room seemed to rock about him and there was thunderous throbbing in his head. He felt as though something had exploded in his brain.

She stood in the doorway between the shop and the room and they exchanged a glance of hatred, Sarah impassive and quite cold, he extremely volatile, unable to keep himself still or to disguise the passionate nausea he felt for her.

He thought he detected in her passivity a trace of a peculiar pleasure, cold and unintelligent, as if it satisfied her sense of greed to stand and do nothing, while he lost his temper and worked himself into an agony. He trembled even more and felt a violent desire to shout at her and stood struggling with his emotions. She seemed to detect his wretchedness and remarked, in a voice of false politeness:

'Oh! go if you wish. There's nothing to stop you.'

He felt he must be logical. He took from his pocket a pound-note and eight shillings in silver. He placed the money on the table by the tea-pot and said:

'You wouldn't like me to be in debt to you.'

'I don't want your money!' she said.

A spasm of alarm crossed her face, her cold expression lessened. He stretched out his hand, pushed the note and the silver towards her without speaking.

'I say I don't want your money!' she cried.

'What's the matter with you?'

'I tell you I want no money from you!'

'Count it and see that it's right.'

'Where are you going?'

'Upstairs.'

'What for?'

'Count it!'

He turned away from her, not troubling to answer, and went upstairs. He heard her repeating in a tone of angry alarm, 'What are you up there for?' but he kept silent. His own angry disgust and his pure reason fused and filled him steadily with an inexorable bitterness. Presently he went downstairs again, determined and calmer, carrying a little leather bag. The expression on her face had grown startled and pitiful and she was holding the money tight in her hands.

'Where are you going?' she said, faintly.

'Got the money?' he cried.

'Yes.'

'Have you counted it?'

'Yes.'

'That's all right then?'

She did not answer.

He placed the bag on a chair and went to the mantelpiece and took down his watch; very deliberately he threaded the chain through his waistcoat and put the watch in the left-hand pocket. It was half-past seven. He picked the bag up again.

She ran to him suddenly with little rapid gestures of her hands and besought him: 'Take the money, take it, take it back again. It ain't the money I want! I don't want no money from you!' Her voice was half-hysterical and her hands sought to press the money into his. He stood impassive, feeling the note and the silver harsh against the skin of his closed hands; he made a sudden gesture with his hands and a silver coin or two fell to the floor and he saw her fall excitedly to her knees; when she scrambled to her feet again her gestures were more urgent and her 'Take it! Take it! It isn't the money I want!' more desperate and pitiful. She tried at last to wrest the bag from his hands, but he gripped the handle coldly and implacably, resisting her until he saw tears rolling down her cheeks and heard her voice piteously insisting:

'It ain't true, is it, it ain't true? It ain't true about her?'

'Yes, it's true,' he said calmly.

'It ain't serious then? You don't want her?'

'Yes, I want her. It's quite serious.'

131

'What am *I* going to do?' she cried.

There was something repulsive to him in her tearful voice and its note of whining entreaty. He remained untouched, only a little fretful and restless, like a man forced to listen to a boring speech. He felt that her tears were artificial. He saw something indecent in her whining grief. He could not prevent this loathing appearing in his face and entering his voice:

'For God's sake get away from me!'

'I won't! Listen to me! Listen to me!'

'Take your hands off this bag!'

She lifted her voice in a sudden tearful rage:

'You're going with that little bitch, eh?'

'With what? With what did you say?' he said.

He advanced on her furiously, wildly incensed by the word.

'What did you say?'

'You heard what I said.'

'Say what you said again.'

They stood glaring at each other, as if awaiting a signal to spring.

'Say it again!' he shouted.

And suddenly she also shouted:

'The little whore, that's what I said! The little whore! The whore!'

As she spoke he felt suddenly a torrent of diabolical fury surge up in him and sweep away his self-control. 'I'll wring your neck!' he shouted in a voice more wildly enraged than ever. He could no longer control his desire for physical violence. He stepped to the table, seized the cup from which he had been drinking, and hurled it without hesitation against the wall behind her. The cup smashed with a terrific noise and Sarah screamed; the fragments of crockery were hurled to the floor and clattered into the sink and the frying-pan, and Sarah's scream seemed also to split up and fly shrilly from wall to wall, repeating itself and filling his head with troublesome echoes. He felt on the verge of hysteria and he was shaking in all his limbs. He wiped his hand across his mouth and his lips were dry and broken, like fragments of bark. He saw Sarah look wildly at the shattered cup strewn in all directions; her eyes were wide, tearful and distracted. He suddenly hated her. He dropped the bag and seized her by the arms and forced her into the chair in which he had been sitting and pressed his hand over her mouth. His strength leapt up with great violence and a temptation to strangle her sprang up in him, but her mouth was weak, soft and wet under his hand, and he felt himself overpowered by a kind of cold pity for her, a pity of detachment. He suddenly released her. She lay with eyes closed. He did not look at her. His hand was wet from her mouth and he wiped it on the table-cloth, slowly and deliberately, with relief. Then he picked up the leather bag and pushed aside the beaded curtain and went into the shop. From the shop, without pausing or looking round, he walked rapidly into the street and down under the railway-arch.

He was still trembling, but his mind felt clear and hard, as if tempered by the enraged heat of his disgust, and he was conscious of easy lightness of spirit, as if the weight of some dark and ugly obligation had been lifted from it for ever.

CHAPTER X

QUINTUS was sitting on a wooden bench in the bar of *The Angel*. He was leaning his head heavily to one side with an air of solemn confidence and was addressing for the third time the man at his side, a little clerk with a white, bland face, a shabby bowler hat and seedy black clothes. Quintus was slightly drunk; his eyes were watery and excited, and he was speaking in a warm, lugubrious voice. His gestures were very flourishing, with a hint of bravado, and at times he almost let fall the large china clock, painted lavishly with nosegays of pink and blue roses, which he was holding proudly in both hands.

He spoke with emphasis and a sleepy smile. 'Ever try your luck on the hoop-la, eh?' he said.

To the rear of *The Angel*, on a piece of waste land, once a paddock, a fair had come to stand. In the breaks of silence between the chink of glasses and the murmur of conversation in the crowded bar, the noise of an organ jingled on the air brassily, playing gay, worn-out airs.

'Ever try your luck on the hoop-la, I say, cocky?'

The man only shook his head.

'Have another drink? Yes?' said Quintus. 'You have another drink and I'll tell you how I won this clock, eh?'

'I should think you're tired of telling me how you won that clock,' said the seedy fellow.

'Ah! but listen. Wait a minute,' said Quintus. 'Wait a minute.' He held the clock against the bowler-hat of his companion, tilting the hat to one side. 'Never heard a clock tick like that all the days of your bloody life, did you?'

The little man made a pretence of listening and nodded his head.

'Should think not! And I'll tell you something else, my old cock sparrow. I'll tell you something else. If you was to put a sovereign down on that table—yes, a sovereign!—I wouldn't part with that clock! I wouldn't *think* o' parting with it. See that?'

The man nodded his head again and took a slow draught of his beer. The bar was thronged with people and a girl with a yellow jumper over a pale green skirt came and sat down on the far side of the table with a glass of wine.

Quintus, in the act of putting the china clock on the table again, became aware of her presence and smiled. His smile was friendly and persuasive and he gave a little gallant wave of his hand.

'See you're looking at my clock,' he said.

'Yes,' said the girl, and she smiled back at him.

He watched her take a tiny bird-like sip at her wine. The little fellow blew his nose on a dirty white handkerchief and winked at her. She wiped her lips delicately with a tiny handkerchief of pale green silk, aloof and unmoved by this effrontery. Quintus stretched out his hand and touched her arm.

'It's a pretty clock, ain't it, eh?' he asked her softly.

'I love the roses all twining up and down it,' she said.

'Here, feel of it,' he urged her. 'Feel of it. Some weight in that, eh? And here, wait a minute, my gal. Listen to it. Hear it! D'ye hear it?'

She pushed away the hair that crossed over her ears and listened with an expression of amused surprise.

'Hear it?' he asked again.

She nodded her head and an expression of blissful joy flooded his face.

135

'Hoop-la!' he said. 'And the damn thing's right too. It's right!'

'Nearly ten o'clock,' she said.

He took the clock from her hands with an air of great solemnity and blew away a dark particle of dust that had settled on the bud of a rose.

'That's a clock fit to stand on the shelf in the living-room of a king,' he declared.

She took another drink of her wine. Her face was thin, pale and attractive and she had a habit of pressing her small red lips together and sucking in the last drops of wine after setting down her glass.

'Listen to me, my gal. I'll tell you how I got that clock.'

'On the hoop-la,' she said quickly. 'I know all about it.'

'Ah! but there's something else,' he told her. 'Something else. You drink that drop of wine and have another glass with me and I'll tell you how I got that clock. Eh?'

She nodded and drank the rest of her wine and wiped her lips again. The seedy fellow, draining his glass also, straightened his bowler-hat and walked away soberly. Quintus ordered some sherry, confiding to the girl in tones of sombre regret:

'Haven't tasted a drop of sherry since my eldest daughter was married. What d'ye think of that?'

She smiled, and when the sherry was brought by the white-aproned barman, she said:

'Well, here's looking at you.'

'You're a nice kid,' he said, holding up his glass, 'damn me if you ain't.'

They drank the sherry together and the wine set Quintus talking again. The speech flowed from his lips in a rapid, excited stream and the words were glib and flowery, like those of an oration.

'Ever try your luck on the hoop-la?' he began. 'Damn

tricky blokes, them hoop-la chaps, cunning as monkeys. They don't lose much. You pay your money and throw your rings, don't you, and when the rings are gone, they're gone, ain't that it? Eh? Ain't that it? Like snipe, them chaps, darting about. Too quick for you. Dirty lot. As lief spit on you as give you the prize when you'd won it. You know that?'

'A soldier I was with once spent ten shillings if he spent a halfpenny and in the end they barred him—turned him clean off,' she said.

'That's it! Turned him off. Crooked humbugs! But I bested 'em, that's something, ain't it? Got this clock out of them anyway. That's something, ain't it? And let me tell you this. It was fair, I won it, the ring went over. See that, don't you? I had my eye on that clock a long time, and I kept ringing and ringing until, thinks I, I'll get that clock if I have to pinch the damn thing. And then'—and he looked at her with a kind of sleepy ferocity, with dark, swimming eyes—'just as I wasn't expecting it, the ring went over pretty as a wedding-ring'd fit on your finger, my gal! Yes! So I called the bloke and I said: "My clock, I think, mate?" "Your clock," he says, "what clock?" "The clock with the pink roses on it," I says, "don't you wash your eyes out?" "Pardon me," he says. Pardon me! Christ! I felt as if I could pull every greasy hair out of his damned head. "Pardon nothing, my cock-sparrow," I says. "You give me that clock before I come over and take it." And then we started like hell! He argued and called me a good fellow and a sportsman and all the sweet names you could think of and tried to make out that that ring hadn't gone clean over. The crowd came round and the folks shouted, but he wouldn't give in. And then I got mad. "If you don't hand that clock over," I says, "I'll smash every damn thing in this stall and you too." "I think not," he says.'

137

'And you rolled into him?'

'Rolled into him? Cocked my leg over the banisters and reached out and tucked that clock under my arm like a young chicken!'

'And what happened?'

'What happened? He reddled like a turkey-cock. That's all. But he never lifted a finger to stop me. Never lifted a finger! He knew I could have eaten him like a fillet of plaice. And my parting words to that man—I'll tell you my parting bloody words to that man. I could see what he was by his damn white face and his greasy black hair. And I saved it up for him. "Dirty bloody Jew!" I yelled at him. What d'ye think of that, eh?'

The girl smiled and nodded her head with a gesture of disgust at the same time, and then, holding the glass delicately, between the tips of her fingers, drained her sherry to the last drop. The lights of the bar shone brilliantly and the curve of her neck was gloriously white.

'Another drink?' said Quintus.

'Look at the time,' she said, and she turned the face of the china clock towards him.

'Late as that?' he said; and then: 'Not going home, my gal?'

'I'll be off now,' she said.

He drank his wine quickly, smacked his lips and with a gesture of tender affection put the china clock under his arm. Having risen also, the girl was looking at the reflection of her pale face in the tall mirror behind the serving-counter; the image was broken up by many bright-coloured bottles standing shelf upon shelf before the glass. She caught a glimpse of her face between a flagon of Italian wine and a bottle of brandy. Quintus caught hold of her yellow jumper and began to insist on her drinking another glass of wine.

But the girl refused; and with Quintus bellowing 'Good

138

night!' to everyone in the crowded bar and muttering at intervals in the girl's ear, 'Well, if you won't drink, you won't drink, but we can walk a little way home together, can't we, eh?' they walked out of *The Angel* into the street.

The October air was sharp and cold and the jingle of the fair-organ and the noise of the fair came in waves of gaiety. Quintus was conscious of a thousand electric lights flickering and dancing and whirling chaotically and he presently began to walk in a line like the coil of a snake. The crowd was very thick and he collided with a drab little woman in a black bonnet holding a saucer of whelks in her hand. There was a fierce altercation, but finally he raised his hat to her. He felt in his heart that this piece of gallantry might be very impressive in the eyes of the girl and he beamed with pleasure.

'Walk through the fair, eh?' he proposed to her.

She shook her head.

'No? Then have a plate of whelks with me?'

'They make me sick,' she said.

She suddenly began to walk up the street. Conscious of being rebuked by her refusals, he walked after her. As they walked along he reeled once or twice in helpless curves; each time he glanced at her, and each time he felt dimly that this behaviour had hardly pleased her. Looking at the misty image of her face, white and silent under the yellow hat, he felt gloomily that he must make amends to her. And suddenly he halted.

'Here, my gal,' he said.

'Yes?'

'If I made you a present of this clock, you'd take it, eh, wouldn't you?'

'You keep the clock yourself,' she said, 'you'd be sorry in the morning.'

'Here, take it,' he urged and half-thrust it upon her.

139

'I don't want it! Your wife'd like a clock like that,' she said.

'Too good for her!' he declared.

'Haven't you got some daughter that's going to be married?' she said.

'No.'

'Haven't you got a daughter?'

'Two,' he said.

'Come along then,' she said. 'You'd be sorry in the morning if you gave a beautiful clock like that away.'

They proceeded along the street again. He carried the china clock under his arm once more. The conversation had sobered him a little and he felt a warm, dreamy gratitude towards the girl for having refused the clock. He felt a desire to treat her to amusing flatteries. And suddenly the pallor and darkness of her face struck him familiarly, and he said:

'I've got a daughter about your clip, my gal.'

'Then you give her the clock,' said the girl. 'What's her name?'

'Pauline. She's the spit of you.'

'That's a nice name.'

'She's a good gal,' he said. 'She's a wonderful good gal. By God, I don't know what we'd do without her. She's twenty-one. We had a party this year, a beautiful party, beautiful party, beautiful.' He ceased speaking on an ecstatic note, suddenly realizing that he had walked almost to Charlotte's Row, within sight of the railway-bridge, and demanded of the girl in a tone of naïve alarm:

'Here, my gal, stop a minute. I ain't drunk, am I?'

'Drunk?' she said. 'If my old dad was never no worse than you are we'd think he was teetotal.'

'I thought I wasn't drunk,' he said.

The girl halted suddenly on the pavement and peered under his arm in order to see the time by the china clock.

140

'You ain't going to leave me?' he said.

'You go home and show that clock to your daughter. She'll love you.'

'Give me a kiss, my gal, eh?' he said. 'You ain't going without giving me a kiss, eh?'

'You kiss your daughter,' she urged. 'You love her, don't you?'

'Love her?' At these words he was conscious of something warm and blissful in his heart. 'Love her?' he exclaimed. 'By God I do!'

'Don't break your clock,' she warned him. 'Good night.'

'Good night, my gal. Good night.'

After she had moved away into the darkness he called after her a little drunkenly, with foolish tenderness:

'God bless you, my gal, God bless you!'

The girl did not reply, and presently he found himself walking under the railway-bridge, the street in blackness before him, the night about him softly silent except for the vague movements of an engine shunting down the line. Just beyond the railway-arch he stopped to look at the china clock again and to listen for its ticking. The tick of the clock was rapid and merry, like the noise of a cricket, and thinking of the girl's words and resolving suddenly to give the clock to Pauline, he was conscious of a desire to behave soberly. He shook his head violently, like a dog, and then wondered momentarily if he should call for a moment at Jonathan's, to show the clock to Masher and talk politics with him until he was sobered again. But he went on, walking the last paces before the dark entry very slowly, spitting at intervals with guttural hawking.

In the entry he groped vaguely for the walls with his hands and walked unhappily in the darkness, with arms outstretched, like a man on a tight-rope. He had slipped the china clock into the poacher's pocket in the lining of his jacket, thinking of bringing it out again like a conjurer in order to dazzle Pauline. Now and then he muttered curses against himself; the dark entry seemed to rock like a ship and his legs seemed to wander off alone, staggering hither and thither, as though no longer part of him.

He reached the yard and there paused, and steadying himself by planting his feet wide apart, contemplated the lighted window. He could hear nothing for one moment but the ticking of the china clock in his pocket.

A second later he heard voices. He advanced and stood under the lighted window and listened. A woman was speaking. The tone was argumentative and occasionally the note of a word was very shrill. He did not recognize the voice and he could not understand the words. In perplexity he tilted back his hat, scratched his head and spat silently.

'Like some damned old starling jangling and wrangling,' he thought, 'whoever she is.'

After a moment he pushed open the door, very quietly, and went in.

The gaslight in the living-room fell white on his face and he blinked rapidly as he entered. The table was laid for supper: a brown stone jar of pickles, a loaf and a piece of red cheese. He saw his wife and Fanny sitting at the table with a bottle of stout between them. They glanced up at him with a startled air as he entered. He stared at them and wiped his mouth with the back of his hand.

At once, instinctively, he looked for Pauline. He felt a spasm of mortification at not seeing her there; he felt also that she ought to have been there, that she might in some way have divined that he was bringing the clock for her. His hand crept to his poacher's pocket and he fingered the face of the clock lovingly and then closed the door.

In that moment he saw Mrs. Jonathan. She was stand-

142

ing so that the open door had hidden her. She was standing with her hands clasped together before her, cold and indifferent, her features set. He regarded her with an air of ironical surprise:

'Visitor, eh?'

Her lips were tightly drawn and her expression of determined sourness never altered. The look in her eyes was aloof and injured and it seemed at any moment as if she would toss her head.

Quintus walked across the room and threw his cap on the sewing-machine. No one moved or spoke: he regarded the three women with a stare of sombre, puzzled intent. There was a long silence, and then suddenly he raised his voice:

'What's the matter with you all, eh?' he cried. 'Am I drunk? Or is this a damn waxworks?'

His wife and Fanny stared at the table-cloth, not speaking. But Mrs. Jonathan spoke in a voice of frigid politeness.

'You're drunk, Mr. Harper,' she said. 'You don't need to tell us that.'

'Oh! that's it, is it?' he said.

'Yes, you're drunk, no doubt of it,' she said.

'That must be why you look so damn beautiful, sour-face,' he retorted.

He smiled lugubriously and she in turn resumed her cool, embittered air. He too became silent. He divined trouble in her presence. Picking up a knife he sliced himself a little triangle of cheese and munched it slowly. Why was she there? He bolted the cheese and wiped his mouth and then tried to make her talk again by remarking:

'Good cheese this. Damn good. Some of yours, eh?'

But she was not to be drawn. Mrs. Harper and Fanny were silent also. He glowered with churlishness from one to the other.

143

At that moment he remembered the china clock. He assumed at once a secretive, pompously ironical air.

'Excuse me a moment,' he said to Mrs. Jonathan. 'Excuse me.'

He fumbled in his pocket; at first he blundered purposely, but once he swayed tipsily from side to side, with curses, unable to help himself. At last he set the clock on the table; its ticking seemed silvery and light in the heavy silence of the room. He waved his hand magnificently.

'There's something for you to gape at!' he exclaimed. 'Beautiful clock, ain't it?'

'Where did you get that clock?' whispered Mrs. Harper, at once suspicious.

He waved his hand again.

'I didn't buy it and I didn't pinch it,' he said. 'But it's mine. It's mine. But I didn't buy it and I didn't pinch it.'

'You've been up to some fine trick somewhere,' she accused him.

'Who says I've been up to some trick?'

'You know you have.'

'Well, that's a damn lie then!' he shouted. 'A damn lie! And I'll tell you summat else. I'm sick o' you women! What's the matter with you all, eh? What d'ye sit here for like a lot o' damn dummies, eh? It makes me sick to look at you—Christ! it makes me sick to look at you.'

'When you've done hollerin' and belchin' yourself hoarse, Mr. Harper,' said Mrs. Jonathan, 'I've summat to say to you that'll make you sick again.'

He regarded her with a stare of hostility and a faint sneer on his lips.

'What's that?' he asked. 'You keep your mouth shut! I don't want to talk to you whatever you got to say.'

He swung his head quickly away from her, angry and contemptuous, and stared with menacing eyes at his wife and daughter.

'Where's Pauline?' he asked swiftly. 'That's what I want to know. Where's Pauline?'

Immediately Mrs. Jonathan leaned abruptly forward over the table, the guides of her thin neck very taut, like wires, her voice as shrill as a quarrelling bird's.

'And that's what we want to know!' she flared. 'That's what we want to know!'

The words took him unawares. He experienced a curious sensation at her repetition of them; they struck through the cloudiness of his drunken mind like bewildering lights flashed upon him from inconceivable angles. He was suddenly at a loss. His mind was stupefied. But still he was not stupefied enough to miss the hint of something dark and menacing in the tone of Mrs. Jonathan's voice.

He did not know what to say. Presently however, gazing at the pink and blue roses of the china clock and remembering his intentions about giving the clock to the girl, he felt a new alarm, a sudden misgiving that something disastrous might have happened to her. He leaned over the table and looked fixedly, his eyes drowsy and afraid, into the faces of Fanny and her mother.

'What's happened to her?' he whispered. 'What's happened to that gal, eh?'

They did not answer, and he was conscious instead of Mrs. Jonathan addressing him again:

'They're frightened to tell you what's happened to her,' she said.

'What's that?' he said. 'What's that you say?'

He suddenly stepped forward and stood face to face with her. He seemed all at once inconceivably tall and powerful and she more than ever thin and cunning, her slightness emphasizing his strength and his manner of crouching like a boxer. The stupidity of his mind was lessening. He was shaking off his drunkenness. He looked into her small eyes with a gaze of sudden hatred, malicious but steady.

'What's that you're saying about that gal, eh?' he growled.

'Don't you belch like that at me!' she flared.

'You be careful I don't wring your damn neck,' he warned her. 'I do what I like here. What about that gal, eh? What about her? Where is she? And why the hell should you know so much about it, anyway?'

Mrs. Jonathan smiled at him with a twist of her mouth. Mrs. Harper leapt to her feet, hurling a fierce injunction at him:

'Why don't you sit down and shut your mouth? You're drunk!'

'I'm drunk, am I? That's all you know. I'm all right. I only want to know about that gal. That's all I want to know.'

'And what makes you suddenly fall over yourself for that, eh?'

'I want to give this clock to her. That's why. That's what I want her for.' He suddenly stared again at Mrs. Jonathan. 'Blast you! What are you laughing at? Eh, woman! What are you laughing at?' he demanded. 'I'll teach you to laugh like that at me!' he shouted. 'Damn you! What are you laughing at, my lady, eh?'

The laugh which had passed over her lips suddenly, faint, angry and sneering, vanished. In its place there appeared a different expression, an unexpected look of ingratiating misery, and she turned her eyes wretchedly on Mrs. Harper and the girl.

'Why don't you stop him?' she cried. 'What can I do against him? You let him stand there, the drunken sod, and say what he likes to me. Why don't you tell him where she's gone? Why don't you tell him?'

'Don't you begin slobbering here!' said Quintus.

146

'Who's slobbering?'

'Never mind that,' he said. 'Where's Pauline? Where is she?'

'You'd like to know, would you?' she half-shrieked. 'You'd like to know?'

'Yes!' he declared. 'I'd like to know.'

She drew herself up and stretched forth her neck and shrieked at him in a voice of half-tearful, half-frenzied rage which completely staggered him:

'She's gone off with my husband! Now belch about that, you humbug!'

He became in that moment as if stunned. His eyes assumed a strange expression, full of a sort of childish suspicion. He gazed slowly at the three women in turn as if they had planned a conspiracy against him. His head seemed thick and heavy once more; he felt for a moment quite drunk again. He lurched forward.

'What's that you're saying?' he said.

'I won't waste my breath on her again, the dirty bitch! You heard what I said.'

The words affected him like a blow; he seized Mrs. Jonathan by the shoulders and began to shout:

'Get out of this house before I wring your damn neck! Out of it! Out of it!'

'Mind what you're doing! Keep your dirty hands off my blouse!'

His fingers were pressing into her flesh like the teeth of a trap. She screamed and began kicking at him with all her force. He cried out with rage and flung her bodily against the wall. At the back of his mind lay the conviction that her words about Pauline were true, but in his rage he felt that she was responsible.

For that he felt an insane desire to punish her, to repay the insult to the girl, to avenge Masher himself for the misery he had endured. He quivered with rage as he

147

looked at her. Her little red eyes were blinking with hatred and she was biting her lip so that she revealed her uneven yellow teeth. For one instant they looked at each other and then, without warning, she spat at him wildly and shouted:

'I'll go out of your damned house when I'm ready. And don't you dare lay a finger on me!'

Mrs. Harper and Fanny sprang to their feet simultaneously. The girl was white and shaking. Mrs. Harper was struggling to speak. But her voice was drowned by the voice of Mrs. Jonathan suddenly screaming unintelligibly as if she had gone mad.

At that moment Quintus, dazed and frenzied by the repetition of her voice, turned to the table and caught sight of the china clock. Without hesitation he seized the clock and hurled it without warning straight at her screaming face. He saw her stoop in terror and he saw the clock burst into fragments of pink and blue as it struck against the wall and her shoulder. He heard the rattle of broken china falling to the floor like a storm of hail and he was conscious a second later Mrs. Jonathan falling also. She staggered and fell as if stunned. And he, as though hypnotized, watched her strike her head on the treadle of the sewing-machine standing in the corner. There was a crash as though of falling iron. The treadle of the machine began to squeak up and down, slowly revolving the wheel, struck into motion by the force of Mrs. Jonathan's head. He saw and heard everything with perfect clearness. But suddenly he felt a strange obscurity, like a faint mist, come over the coloured fragments of china, the sewing-machine slowly rocking itself to stillness, and the figure of Mrs. Jonathan lying like a heap of old clothes, still and huddled, with her face to the floor. He stood motionless, staring down at all this, feeling suddenly as though it were all part of his drunkenness. And he felt that there was something strange and drunken about his wife's voice also, repeating some words which seemed to reach him from the end of a gigantic room:

'You'll go to prison for this, you damn fool, you'll go to prison for this!'

CHAPTER XI

ADAM was aroused one morning in January by the gaunt figure of his grandmother standing over the bed with a candle in her hand. He became aware in a dreamy way of her bony hand shaking his shoulder, her old, cracked voice telling him smartly: 'Slip into your things; it's half-past six,' and then of the cold vacant room and the candle which she had left burning before the white face of the clock standing by the bedside. Getting up, pulling on his cold trousers over his warm, sleepy legs, and feeling the ice-cold air take its vicious sweeps at him through the cracks at the window, he felt half-blind with sleep and oppressed by wretchedness, as though being driven to something against his will. He was conscious of hating the naked ticking of the clock and the cold white stick of candle burning unsteadily. And all this seemed only to emphasize the silent, freezing winter morning darkness, which he hated above all.

As he went downstairs, carrying the candle in his hand, he saw a light in the lodger's room and he remembered in that moment why he was made to get up in the darkness. At the foot of the stairs he blew out his candle and went into the lodger's room with the wick still smoking its grey thread before his face. He saw his grandmother. Her hair was knotted roughly like a bunch of thistledown, and she was bending over the bare deal table in the centre of the room, hastily cutting slices of bread. A candle was burning on the breakfast-table beside a black tea-pot, a pot of dripping and a blue packet of sugar spread out on a sheet of newspaper. The room was bare and cold and he could see through the windows a handful of stars shining in the dark bluish square of morning sky like a glitter of frost.

His grandmother lifted her head and brushed back a coil of straggling hair with her hand and spoke quickly:

'Why don't you make haste? Where are your shoes? Do you want the baker to send you back home the first morning you get there?'

'Where are my shoes?' he said.

'Where you left them!'

In that half-blind, still almost sleeping state he could not remember where he had taken off his shoes. He groped and stooped about the room in a dazed way, his sensation of misery and sleepy hatred increasing. Occasionally, forgetting his boots, he thought only of the words the old woman had just spoken. The thought that he was going to work for the baker repeated itself miserably in his mind. Stupefied and increasingly unhappy, he half gave up the search for his boots; but suddenly the old woman whispered half-angrily at him:

'Are you going to be all day finding your shoes?'

He made a pretence of looking for his boots again, not speaking. She watched him pitilessly as he groped about the floor in the half-darkness.

'Under the cot,' she rapped out at last. 'In a minute they'll bite you.'

Under the child's cot standing in the corner by the window he caught a stale sour odour of sickness. He found his boots and dragged them on his feet and knelt on the floor to lace them up. There were other boots standing in a row along the skirting-board by the bed; they were the boots of the lodger and his wife, and the candlelight gleamed on their worn brass eyelets until it seemed as if they were staring at him from so many pairs of steadfast, forlorn eyes.

151

They had been living together in the single room since Christmas; the lodgers, the boy and his grandmother. The boy had hated to sacrifice the privacy of the kitchen for the colder, larger room that looked out on the street, with its door opening straight to the pavement, its bitter draughts, its cold, naked walls, the strange odour of the child's sickness.

'Why do we live in there with them?' he had asked.

'Because it's better, that's why?'

'Why is it better?'

'The boy's short of work and he can't afford the rent. We burn half the fire in there and half the light. So it's better for all of us.'

He understood this explanation and accepted it. He was aware perfectly of what it all meant. But he continued to hate the change; he felt a loss of pride, a loss of independence. Poverty had utterly triumphed over them and they had meekly surrendered.

He laced up his boots with savage misery, his hands already stiff with the coldness of the room. When he had finished he came straight to the table and watched his grandmother spreading a slice of bread with oily yellow dripping. So early in the morning he did not expect that he must wash himself. Expectantly he waited for the bread and dripping, hoping that the old woman would deal leniently with him. But she turned on him smartly even as the knife flashed across the bread :

'And now make haste and wash your eyes out! If you're going to the baker's you're going clean, let me tell you. And no licking, my son. Get the dust out of your eyes and dry your ears clean.'

She hustled him from the room. He felt in that moment as if she were utterly inhuman and purposely cruel to him. Hard with misery against her he went into the kitchen, drew a little water in the blue enamel bowl and tried to wash himself. The soap, yellow and stiff as frozen clay, slipped from his numb fingers when he tried to use it and the water was icy, like death, and he was afraid of it, cringing from the touch of it, hating the thought of plunging in his face. He splashed about a little, puffing and snorting in pretence, and then rubbed his face with the towel, wiping the dust from his eyes and ears.

In the act of doing this he suddenly heard a deathly, whooping sound of coughing from the lodger's bedroom. The baby had grown pitifully white and sunken, like a skeleton. It was difficult to believe that such a frail creature could produce this hollow, desperate, powerful whoop, like the cough of a horse, without ever resting. He listened to the sound filling the house, with now and then a more desperate whoop as the child fought for breath; and then against this sound he heard a fainter coughing, dry, harsh, rattling, almost like a stifled echo of the other.

He went into the lodger's room and found his grandmother standing by the fireplace, fighting for breath. Her face had the strange bluish pallor which had often made him afraid. Her lips were deeply blue. He heard the curious whistling in her throat and saw her lips helplessly dribbling the hateful yellow phlegm.

She looked at him searchingly, in a pitiful way. She tried to speak to him, but her words seemed to be strangled, and she only gave a little cry like a weasel and fell to spitting again. All this time the coughing of the child also went on, so that the sounds flung themselves one against the other, as though mocking each other.

When her coughing had ceased the old woman dropped into a chair and said to him in a curious, deathly whisper:

'Now go to the baker's. Go along, I tell you. Take a piece of bread-and-dripping and go along. Do as I tell you.'

He looked at her thin yellow face, suffering but inexorable. He knew that there was nothing he could do but take the slice of bread and depart.

Wretched and alarmed and feeling also for the second time that she was behaving cruelly towards him, he went out into the frozen darkness of the yard. The sky was cloudless and sprinkled with myriads of stars, like shining particles of ice; nevertheless it seemed strangely, everlastingly dark, and there was a feeling as if the dawn would never break above the crowded roofs shining dimly with frost. He walked slowly along the yard, eating the bread. His boots rang clearly on the frozen ground, creating such echoes that he was overcome by a sensation that he alone was awake, perhaps even alive, in a world made up of silent black houses, infinite coldness and the scattered, impersonal, far-off stars.

He stood still for a moment at the Harpers' yard. When he stood utterly still there was no sound, so that it then seemed to him like a world of the dead. He did not often go into the Harpers' now; he could never go past the house without remembering acutely that Pauline was no longer there. And now the lock was always on the door of the shop. Quintus had gone to prison for quarrelling with Mrs. Masher. In the winter morning starlight the place seemed uninhabited and dead. It meant nothing to him. He stood eating his bread dreamily, wondering solemnly if Quintus would ever come back. As he stood there a candle was lighted in the bedroom overlooking the yard and he saw the figure of a woman passing vaguely to and fro in the room. He immediately thought of Pauline, asking himself over and over where she had gone, why there was no news of her, if she would ever return. He recalled the days when they had often been together, the church on Easter Sunday, the warm, beautiful day when they had fished in the stream with Masher. His mind returned also to the peep-show they had made and the words about his mother came back to him swiftly. A curious sense of sorrow and awe overcame him then, a sensation sharp and poignant, as if she were still with him, almost as if she were still part of his life, his flesh and his spirit, even though he could not remember her. Odd fragments of her life, ingrained with terrible depth upon his mind, reiterated themselves in his consciousness through the voice of Pauline, and the loss of the girl became bound up, in some incomprehensible way, with the loss of his mother.

He stood watching the candlelight and the shadow; his finger-tips were numb; he could hardly feel the bread. His wretchedness hung upon him heavily as he continued to walk down the yard, past the black, silent houses, into the street. There was still no sign of dawn. The air was so cold that it seemed as if the stars must be thawed before the light could come. And again he hated the intense coldness, the darkness and now above all the thought of going to work for the baker. The necessity of it all maddened and humiliated him and made him afraid. He felt that it would be unbelievably beautiful not to go. He suffered in anticipation, cold with fear.

As he approached the steps to the bakehouse and set his feet on the lowest of them, he saw the blue-and-orange flare, turned very low and now more blue than orange, casting its faint light on the windows covered with flour-dust. He remembered that he had wanted to work for the baker a year ago. Now the sickliness of this blue flame reminded him suddenly of the sick, blue colour of his grandmother's face. He stood still. He knew that she would die. And standing there with his hand ready to grasp the great brass knob of the door he suffered the acutest misery of all; he visualized for one moment not only a world in which she did not exist, but a world also to which Pauline and Masher and Quintus, all the people he loved and cherished, would return no more.

Never quite losing his hatred of it all, and often miserable with loneliness and fear, he continued to work for the baker throughout the winter. He went to the bakehouse every morning before seven and again every evening at five, returning home after darkness.

The baker gave him a shilling a week and he helped at first to carry the loaves and flour to the cart and break up the salt for the bread. Sometimes he also helped to fodder the horse; this meant going up a vertical ladder to the dark loft above the stable and throwing down hay and straw into the stall below. The ladder was old and rickety and he was terrified while ascending it and doubly terrified when coming down again. It seemed inevitable that the weight of his body should wrench the ladder away from the wall and that he would fall and crush himself on the bricks below. The bakehouse was small and dim and the windows were covered thickly with flour-dust. Two large ovens and a furnace blocked out the entire space of one wall. It was always warm and stifling in there, and the lower oven, when opened, seemed to him like the cave of some monster. When the gas-flare was lighted and swung on its long arm into the oven, the light and shadow playing on the burnt walls, the roof and the shining iron floor littered with breadcrumbs was grotesque and uncanny.

The baker's name was Zachariah Corday. Adam was warned by his grandmother to respect him. He was a Strict and Particular Baptist and he never baked on Sundays. Adam went to work for him with a sort of reverential fear in his heart, believing in him and trusting him, awed into a silent meekness and duty by the thought of his godliness. He was a tall, very thin man; his face was hollowed and white, with a deathly look about it, as if the flour-dust had eaten into it year after year and would

156

never wash away again. His mouth had been worn thin and hard, until something avaricious, unkind and hypo-critical lurked about it, even when he smiled. His clothes also were white with flour-dust and he shuffled about the bakehouse all day in a pair of shabby carpet-slippers tied on by pieces of string, his white apron flapping loosely about his legs, his movements weary and apathetic, creat-ing altogether an impression of something poor and sick, like a worn-out horse. He got up very late in the mornings and regularly read the Bible over his breakfast in the shabby living-room and then went to see if the furnace was alight with the Bible still in his hands. He pretended to trust a great deal in Providence and the bread-round did not begin until early evening. Sitting in a black covered-in van drawn by a small weak brown horse, the baker and Adam would drive in desultory fashion about the poorest streets of the town, the boy taking charge of the pony while the baker went slowly from house to house with the basket. As the autumn came on it was often chilly in the cart and they would drive home in darkness, the cart-lamps shining with an unsteady orange light on the drooping back of the horse.

On these journeys the baker rarely spoke to him and in the bakehouse he treated him as something automatic and impersonal. He asked for things to be done sharply, in a barking voice, and he kept a queer, indirect kind of watch on the boy until he had finished. As time went on he demanded an increasing amount of work, and the boy was never still. He returned home with a weariness in his chest and limbs which hitherto he had never known. On Saturdays he worked all day, polishing the cart-lamps and oiling the harness in the mornings, cleaning the stable in the afternoon and going on the bread-round as usual in the evening. The cart-lamps were heavy and he hated the work, a miserable bitterness smouldering in his heart. The

157

stable was foul with urine and dung, and the sodden manure on the long stable-fork strained his strength. At first he was afraid of being kicked by the horse. But gradually this fear passed and he taught the horse gently to step over when he wished it and he grew fond of the pleasant silkiness of its flank and of its satin lips seeking his hand.

After he had worked for the baker a week or two the horse came to know him and they grew fond of each other; and on Saturdays the baker's wife made it a practice to give him a loaf of bread. She tucked it into his hand half-secretly and during the week she often gave him twists of bread, darkly baked and very sweet, and a cake or two. She was a plump, fair-haired woman with gay blue eyes. She had a strange habit of catching young mice by their tails and throwing them high into the air and shrieking with laughter as they fell and crushed themselves in the yard below. The boy liked her. She drank a little in secret and was fond of bright clothes and flirted with the man who called with the yeast. After a little flirtation she would allow his hand to creep to her bosom and he would tell her stories in a kind of deathly whisper that made her go off into a series of suppressed giggles, as if he were tickling her.

He worked at the bakehouse throughout the winter. The time seemed endless. But soon the first lent-lilies came into the shops and there were a few slender narcissi, fresh as snow, with the eye of the sun burning soft and red in them. In the early evenings there was often a clear, virgin light in the sky and in the gardens of the big houses, sheltered by fir trees, which the boy and his grandmother passed as they went home from the bird-shop, there were snowdrops blooming, colder and paler in their loveliness than anything on earth.

In March there was talk of Pauline. His grandmother

and his great-aunt talked of her one Sunday evening while he sat engrossed in looking at a case containing a pike, hanging over the door leading to the stairs.

'And by the way, what about that girl? Where is she now?'

'That's a long tale. She went to live with Masher in London. You knew that. Well, Masher tried to get a job here and a job there but nothing ever came right. And then she tried to get a job and she got some work at a dressmaker's. She was used to a machine. They had rooms in a basement, and I think a man who sold books, a socialist or somebody, let them have the room and he let Masher have books to read as well, and the end of it was that Pauline worked and kept them both. That's all I know. And that was two months ago.'

Beyond this he heard nothing. Easter came near and he remembered her vividly. He wondered if she would ever return and he had misgivings lest she should have forgotten him if she did return.

The winter lingered, but now the shops were never empty of daffodils and there were primroses in the sheltered spots beyond the town. The lodgers still did not pay their rent in full and the baby continued to be sickly.

With Quintus in prison the Harpers went deeper into debt; they could no longer shop at Jonathan's and it was difficult to find credit elsewhere. Two of the sons married and left home. George, the one-eyed brother, began to give lessons on the euphonium in his bedroom, taking two pupils a week, charging a shilling per lesson of an hour. Fanny went into the factory in Pauline's place and Mrs. Harper closed boot-uppers in the kitchen, on the sewing machine.

When Easter was three weeks away Adam waited one morning as usual in the bakehouse for the loaf to be given him. It was half-dark in the bakehouse, only the blue jet

159

at the oven burning in the warm stillness. He could hear the baker wheeling the cart under the shed in the yard and then the tinkle of harness and the sound of hoofs, first on the bricks and then in the straw, as the horse was led away. He waited, quite still, and presently he saw that it was dark also in the living-room, and he felt instantly that the baker's wife would not come. He tip-toed and looked into the room; it was empty. He could see the white clock-face shining in the darkness. The thought that for the first time he would go away without the loaf filled him with a strange, sickening feeling of dismay. Some words he had so often used in mere earnestness sprang through his mind, savage and desperate in their beseechment: 'Please God, don't let her forget the bread.' He stood still in the middle of the bakehouse and listened again. There was no sound from the yard and only a faint murmur in the furnace and the beating of his own heart. The blue flame of the gas-jet, straight as a finger, burned steadily and soundlessly. He could see the sky through the windows, motionless, vague, without stars, and across the floor lay a faint, steadfast crimson glow thrown from the furnace, falling on the flour bins and his own feet.

A long time seemed to pass and he was conscious very sharply of the utter emptiness of the house about him. He saw objects in the bakehouse itself more clearly, the bags of flour, the blocks of salt piled up in rows against the wall, the peels suspended against the ceiling and lastly the loaves themselves. His eyes rested upon the loaves with longing. The loaves were stacked one above another, impossible to count. He gazed at them with anxiety, gradually obsessed by them until he forgot the empty house, the baker, the light from the gas-jet and even himself in watching them. As he gazed at them a strange nervousness seized him, a feeling of desperation mingled with guiltiness.

The silence remained unbroken, and he felt as if he were alone on earth. Suddenly this feeling of utter solitude, mingled with his fear, made him start forward to the table and touch the bread. The loaves felt fresh and crisp under his hands, the fragrance of the bread came up to him sweetly, and suddenly he seized a loaf in his hands.

As soon as his hands had closed about the bread he was afraid again. He tried to hide the loaf under his jacket and then he half-ran to the door and stopped and tried to hide the loaf a second time. Then he heard a sound, and terror ran through his heart and he stood trembling. There were footsteps in the yard and he stood petrified between a desire to put back the loaf with the rest and a longing to run away.

But he did not move and the door opened. The baker walked in. In his terror the boy dropped the bread, and the loaf went bounding about the floor, the stiff crust cracking on the bricks, pink in the firelight.

The boy felt a queer sensation of weakness in his limbs. The baker stood motionless, holding the door half-open in his hands, gazing at the fallen loaf while in turn the boy fixed his eyes on him. There was a brief silence, and then the baker suddenly swooped across the bakehouse and picked up the loaf and confronted the boy.

'What were you doing with this?' he whispered horribly. 'What were you doing with this?'

Terror surged through the boy and swept away his senses. He only stood silent, looking at the baker.

'What were you doing with this loaf, I say? What were you doing? Answer me. What were you doing? What were you doing?'

Again the boy did not speak. Suddenly, as if enraged by his silence, the baker began banging the loaf against his head, dealing the blows in rapid succession before the boy could move or raise his hands. The blows knocked him against the table and he was dazed. Before he could recover the baker rushed at him swiftly again, his voice unsteady with anger. Again and again he dealt the boy blows with the loaf so that the boy tumbled like a ninepin. At last, in struggling to his feet, he felt the baker kicking him, half-helping him to his feet with the force of the blows.

'Get up off the floor! Get up, can't you! Get up!' he shouted.

The boy staggered to his feet. There came a torrent of angrier words:

'That will teach you not to take things which are not your own! That will teach you! Who said you could have the loaf? Did I say you could have it? What have you got to say about it? What have you got to say? You were going to steal it, weren't you? Answer me that. You were going to steal it, wern't you? Weren't you?'

The boy, not answering, began to run to the door.

'And is this the first time?' the baker shouted. 'If I thought you'd laid a finger on a loaf I'd knock you flat, do you hear me, I'd knock you flat, you plague, until the wickedness of the devil was driven out of you and you knew better! And you shall know better! Do you hear me? You shall know better!'

The boy had reached the door leading to the yard while the baker was speaking. He opened the door and began to run in a dazed, uncertain fashion across the yard. He heard the baker throw down the loaf and in his terror of pursuit he ran wildly, not knowing which way to turn for escape. He heard the man running behind him, and he felt that he had no chance of escape. Sooner or later he must be run to earth like a rabbit, and beaten again.

His only chance of eluding the baker even momentarily was the stable. The bolt of the door was stiff and he only managed to unbolt the door and run inside as the baker came up with him. Inside however he felt at once a sense of protection and relief. The smell of straw and dung comforted him and the presence of the horse reassured him like a blessing. Dimly, like a shadow against the white-washed walls, he could see the horse outlined, its familiar form still and friendly. He felt suddenly less afraid of the baker. The horse stirred at the noise he made and the boy threw himself down in the shadow between the horse and the wall, away from the door.

He tried not to breathe or even to tremble. A moment later the baker came into the stable, stooping a little, and as if he knew instinctively where the boy was lying he strode through the straw to him, without a word, and wrenched him to his feet. The boy tried to struggle, but it seemed as if his shoulders were held in an iron trap, and when he tried to sink to the ground it was as though he were held by a rope in the air. He could hear the baker's breathing as it hissed through his teeth, and suddenly he felt himself being shaken violently to and fro like a rat in anger. His outstretched hands touched the flank of the horse. Restless at the commotion, the horse moved over in the straw.

It was very dark in the stable but the boy knew instinctively when the baker took down the horse-whip. Although his senses and his body were numb with fear he recognized the thin whine of the lash as it came through the air and he felt the first blow of it on his back as if his clothes had already been stripped from him. The whip came upon him like a hot wire. It must have curled in the darkness like a serpent. After feeling the lash once or twice the boy did not know how often the baker struck him. He knew merely that he struck him quickly, viciously, always in silence except for the hissing sound of his breath between his teeth. Sometimes the fierce pain of the lash caused him to droop to the ground, and then the baker would use the handle of the whip on him, prodding him until he stood upright again. At the first stroke of the lash he cried out and each blow seemed to strike fresh tears from him, until his face was wet and salt with weeping. He felt he must cry out with all his strength against the pain. But the sounds that he made were weak with terror. He knew that they would never be heard. Gradually he cried only within himself, appealing instinctively to the far-off, tender figure of his mother. At last the face of his mother seemed to stoop over him, pale and tender, oddly confused with the face of Pauline, bearing a strange resemblance to the girl which struck through his pain and misery with a mysterious joy that was like a pain also, stinging deep into his soul. At last the face of his mother seemed to change into the loaf he had tried to steal and the loaf began steadily to fall into his eyes until it covered him like a shadow. He struggled briefly and ineffectually, as he had struggled against the baker. Finally the loaf struck him and he was conscious of falling into darkness.

He heard the dim voice of the baker still half-ordering, half-appealing to him:

'Get up off the floor! Get up, can't you? Get up! What are you lying there for? Get up! Get up!'

He tried to obey the voice, which grew gradually dimmer. He was terrified of the consequences of disobeying. But he could not rise, and suddenly he felt his hands sink away into the wet straw, and he let the darkness cover him.

CHAPTER XII

QUINTUS came out of prison on the day before Easter; there was a pure yellow light in the air and crystal-white angles of frost were lying in the shadows of the houses, braided wet and black at the edges where the spring sunshine had touched; the sky was blue and tranquil and there was a feeling in the air of spring and holiday together. Quintus instantly remembered similar mornings, when he had taken a dog and had walked out into the country in order to see the hounds meet in the little stone villages he knew so well among the woods. He was very fond of the hunt. He would often follow all day on foot; his powerful body never tired. He loved both dogs and horses slavishly, possessed of that curious tenderness of feeling for animals which often redeems mere physical brutishness. At the sight of the hounds with their host of quivering tails and the light, prancing motion of their sinuous white bodies eager to start the run, he would be filled with a strange excitement, so that he could not rest until the dogs had begun their bounding and crying along the ridings and among the trees. In prison he had longed desperately for a dog. He liked to clasp the head of a dog between his knees and press its ears softly back and gaze softly and steadfastly into its eyes. He had missed his dogs miserably and bitterly. And he would wonder if they had been properly fed. Or if they would remember him. Or he was fretted by the thought that they might have been sold or had perished in the long weeks of frost.

He walked into the heart of the town; it was market-day and people were thick on the pavements, like silly flies. Some red cattle lumbered into the street, in a panic of disorder, fouling the pavement, terrified by the hooting of cars and the crowd of humanity on all sides. A beast halted in the road and bellowed; women ran in all directions. Quintus stood still, unable to pass. Jostled and sick of the noise and the crowd, he kept thinking savagely: 'No sooner do I want to put my damn foot down than somebody else must get there first. Give me a stick and a little dog afore this and let me be in a wood where I won't be trampled on.'

He felt he must get out of the town, into a day of pure freedom. But he had no dog. And without a dog he would be lonely and could do nothing. A dog was everything. 'Not so much of your damn people for me,' he often said. 'There's people as'll skin a flint for a farden, but a dog's different. You don't catch a dog up to them monkey tricks.'

The thought of the woods and the dog troubled him continuously. He felt morose and faintly bitter, but he continued to wander aimlessly about the streets, though he hated them, his whole manner careless and detached and faintly bewildered.

He realized clearly that he could go home for the dog. But he did nothing. The notion of home produced a succession of bitter thoughts, above all the thought that he was not wanted there. From the first he had known that his offence was looked upon by the family with a kind of angry satisfaction. He had thrown his weight about once too often, and they were glad. He had bullied and wasted often enough without a finger laid on him in reply, but now they could see him punished, put in his place, subdued at last. He never forgot the police-court, where no one had breathed a single word in praise or defence of him. During the whole proceeding he knew that everyone was thinking, 'Let him go and good riddance. What

do we care? Can't we get along without *him*?' All this
had infuriated him. 'Two can play at that game,' he
thought. 'They'll be damn lucky if they ever see me
back again.' But secretly he knew he would go back, if
only for a certain sneaking pleasure in watching the effect
on them. At the bottom of his heart, however, existed a
suspicion of fear, too. Where was Pauline? What had
happened? And there sprang up also the old antagonism
against Mrs. Jonathan. He had never ceased to hate Mrs.
Jonathan bitterly. He had never wavered from the conviction that she was the cause of it all. Had she never
been a cold, avaricious, mean-souled bitch, Masher would
never have left her, Pauline would never have gone away
and there would have been no prison for him. All his
confused attempts to understand Masher and the girl,
his fears for her and his occasional resentment against
Masher would end alike, all consumed and forgotten in
the violence of his hatred for the woman. He felt that
another clock at her head would be good for her, and he
felt as before that his only remorse would come from
breaking the clock. He had never hated prison as much
as he hated Mrs. Jonathan. But he could do nothing
against her. And he was aware of his helplessness. He
was like a man in a box; he could only fling himself at
the walls and hurt himself.

It was eleven o'clock as he came into the market-place.
Long parallel rows of stalls stood on the cobbled square:
there was a feeling of activity everywhere and a smell of
fruit and produce in the air. He had already made up his
mind not to go home until darkness, and there was a
curious, heavy inertia upon him at the thought of the
empty day before him. He felt desperately that he must
do something. The day must be ordered. It was as though
the function of imprisonment had not ceased.

'I'll get a drink,' he thought.

167

In the bar, while waiting to be served, he looked at his face in a mirror which advertised whisky in silver and scarlet lettering behind the counter. In his face lurked something hard and sombre, with a flash of hostility mingled with furtiveness; his eyes were unflickering and metallic, like two polished bullets in a face that was strangely hard and robust, without the fleshy, dissolute look of old. His eyes stared resentfully, as though he hated even his own questioning look at himself. His body had changed too: his shoulders were squarer and sharper and his clothes seemed to sit awkwardly upon the raw heavy bones; there was less flesh on him and a certain tightness in his frame, though when the beer came he lounged forward on the woodwork with the habitual powerful brooding attitude of the shoulders, so that he looked more than ever like some old tough boxer.

He knew that imprisonment had changed his face and he was glad to look away from the mirror. He drank quickly and came out into the market-place with the beer still wet on his lips. Coming out he took off his cap, scratched his head quickly and tugged on the cap again. He wore it at an angle, slightly backward, flat against his right ear. His hair had been cropped close and the scalp shone white as though powdered with salt under the new black hair.

He thrust his hands into the tops of his trousers, in the tightness made by his black leather belt against his stomach, and spat on the cobbles and walked down an aisle of the market, among the fishmongers. The beer had made him feel different and he felt some of his bewilderment and stiffness fall away.

Nevertheless his mind suffered still from a kind of cramp. He needed activity. He was hungry for something to occupy him. At the same time he was heavy with a curious lassitude: the flesh was willing but the spirit poor and weak. He wandered about from stall to stall, careless, perfectly composed, a little contemptuous, only pausing sometimes to stare at the fruit piled up in gold and green and scarlet pyramids in the spring sunshine. He liked also to stand before the white and green piles of vegetables and the shining banks of flowers. There were thousands of daffodils huddling their cold, yellow, virgin faces close together, snow-white narcissi with the pheasant's eye, early pink and white tulips, the petals shining and silken in the clear light, and sheaves of wallflowers, splashed with gold and blood, and pots of delicate things of china-blue, like fragile bells, whose names he did not know.

The flowers recalled Masher. He began to think of Pauline too. At the first thought of her he almost ran home merely to see if she had returned. Her absence hurt him: he was numb with a misery new to him whenever he remembered she had gone away. Since she had shown a spirit of antagonism against him he had found himself driven to admiration and then to love of her. Consciously he had never loved his children. But now with Pauline it was different. She was a good girl, she had spirit, and perhaps she would never come back. The uncertainty of not knowing whether she had returned made him writhe with misery. Why had she gone away? Wasn't the house good enough for her? Was she ashamed? But he was incapable of reasoning out an answer and he was only bitter with love for her.

Suddenly he was hungry. He bought himself a pound of red apples, stuffing them loose in his roomy pockets. He ate one with great, cracking bites and while eating it came into an aisle where pet animals and birds were sold.

There were cages of white terrier puppies, some blue hares and a few white, silk-haired rabbits with beautiful pink eyes, mild and sleepy with languor. Among the birds there were pigeons, bright green budgerigars and canaries which quivered with agitation on their thin perches, their slender bodies shining lemon and gold in the sunlight. The air was full of the noisy barking of dogs and the birds' pretty twittering and singing.

Quintus halted and became at once fascinated. He stood before the bird-cages with one hand beneath his belt, his body thrown slightly backward, the other hand twanging and scratching the bars. The birds sang to him and threw back their proud, insignificant golden heads and fluttered about the cages in a kind of half-ecstatic, half-distressed excitement. He felt happy. Occasionally he put forward his head and whistled softly to them in return; or he pressed his lips together and made a curiously sweet, enticing sound and said:

'Rattle away, my beauties!'

He remained for a long time whistling and talking to the birds. The little white terriers were lean, cowed and pathetic, not dogs at all, but the canaries, with their long, frantic singing, carried him away. He hesitated before a tiny, slender bird, wonderfully yellow, with a blush of green, like the half-unfastened bud of a daffodil.

He found the stall-keeper and enquired:

'What are the canaries?'

'Cock or hen?' the man asked quickly.

Quintus pointed with his thumb to his canary. The man was quick and darting, like a small dark bird himself.

'What's that little joker?' said Quintus.

'That little cock. Let you have it for seven-and-six,' he said.

It was cheap enough, but he had hoped for less. He took a closer look at the bird; it was a fine, beautifully coloured cock. If Pauline had come home it would sing for her; she would have no cause to say that the home was drab again.

'Cage an' all?' he said.

170

'Yes! cage an' all. Take it?'

Quintus moved away without a word. The faintest air of contempt hung about him again and the stall-keeper flung after him quickly:

'It's no bloomin' yellow-hammer painted up, let me tell you that.'

'Who said anything about it?' drawled Quintus.

'It's a beautiful cock, that's all I'm telling you. Norwich-bred bird, outdoor, just on full song. It's worth it, ain't it?'

'Not to me it ain't.'

'You go to a shop and they'll charge you that for some damned old hen that can't sing pussy. Now that bird *can* sing. You know that.'

'Sings a bit,' said Quintus, poking the bars.

'A bit! That bird'll be singing when you're dead!'

'Not it.'

'Well, *hark* at it! Ain't that singing?'

The bird was singing flashily, in a momentary ecstasy. Quintus acknowledged it by spitting on the cobbles. The bird was really beautiful.

But the price was hopeless. He began to walk away again. He walked past the rows of canaries and the cages of dogs before the stall-keeper called:

'Tell you what I'll do. Let you have it in a cheaper cage for a dollar.'

Quintus came slowly back, as though unwillingly, not showing the excitement he felt. The bird was cheap. He loved it already. The cage did not matter; no bird could live in that tiny mouse-trap of a cage.

So he paid for the bird and put the cage under his arm.

'And you've got a beautiful bird, a bird as'll never stop singing.'

Quintus nodded, and very pleased with himself said with solemn wit:

171

'One thing I want to ask you. Is it temperance? Will it die if I take it in a pub for half an hour?'

He carried the bird about with him all day, till evening. He had bought the bird, not for himself, but for Pauline, and often this caused him to solicit admiration for it passionately in the bars where he sat and passed the time. And this time there was no falsity, no humbug, as with the china clock, about his intentions. He was sober. He loved the girl. And the bird must be worthy of her.

When evening came on he walked steadily home in a blue clear twilight. Under his arm the canary was silent, as though worn out. Some women hurried past, hugging daffodils to their breasts, and vanished into a church. The windows were pale candlelight and the cold, mystic feeling of Easter came to life definitely.

He put aside the feeling that he was not wanted at home. The thought of the girl and the canary under his arm made him bold, until he was eager to step into the familiar kitchen again. He could hear a church bell ringing as he walked up Charlotte's Row. He walked into the yard and stepped into the kitchen quietly, a trifle subdued in manner, blinking in the gaslight. Mrs. Harper was sitting alone in the room. A bright fire was burning and a man's grey shirt was airing on a wooden horse in the fender.

It was his own shirt. So she had expected him. They exchanged glances.

'So you've come?' she said.

'H'm,' he answered.

He set the canary on a chair unobtrusively. Her remark was detached and a little cold, and he knew at once that she was hardly glad he had come. Yet she had prepared for him and she was plainly disturbed by the sight of him too.

He took off his cap. It was a habit of years that he

should fling his cap, with a deft throw like a quoit-player, on the sewing-machine in the corner. But to-night the sewing-machine was not there, and he frowned, troubled by its absence and by the odd sense of space it gave to that part of the room. He continued to stand up, staring.

'There's a chair,' said Mrs. Harper.

'I can stand,' he said.

'Well, it's your legs you wear out, not mine.'

At that he came towards the fire, a trifle meekly. He saw her look at the canary, which had aroused itself again in the warm room.

'Did they give you that?' she asked with the faintest sarcasm.

'Give me what?'

'What made you buy a thing like that if they didn't?' she asked. 'A canary!'

'Never do you mind!'

He sat down vigorously. The old tone of their relationship had already been struck perfectly again; the bickering, unfriendly, mistrustful contempt for each other, almost a habit, showed itself at once as if the prison had never intervened. Only the clean shirt was a symbol of tenderness, a sign that there ever was, or ever could be, something finer between them.

He sat in silence. She looked with wonder at his hardened, fleshless face, his cropped head clean and shining as a pebble. He in turn was puzzling over the missing sewing-machine. Now and then the canary fluttered along its perch, chirruping briefly.

'Do you want anything to eat?' she said.

'What have you got?' he asked.

'That's a nice way to speak!' she flashed. 'Did you lose *all* your manners in quod?'

'I did,' he said.

She rose irritably, banged about from kitchen to pantry,

173

spread a cloth, and brought out a portion of a loaf, a piece of cheese and some cold sausage. Everything looked stale and poor. It was a mere ghost of a meal. Even when in debt the Harpers had always eaten well and he could not understand this paltry meal which she was setting before him.

'Won't be twelve baskets of crumbs from this show,' he said.

'Be thankful for what you do get!' she flashed.

She sat down again with a flat air of 'take it or leave it' which did not escape him, and withdrew into silence. He began to eat alternate hunks of cheese and sausage on thick oblongs of bread. He set the canary on the table among the crocks and made the sweet half-whistling sound to it with his pursed lips. Once he rolled pellets of bread and then of cheese and tried to feed the bird through the bars.

'Yes, I should think you're going to waste good food on a pet bird!' she flashed at once.

'What's a matter, woman? What's a matter?' he asked in slow astonishment. 'What's a mossel o' bread one way or another? What's a crumb or two?'

'A good lot—to us!'

He remembered the time, before the house painter had moved in, when their neighbours had kept pigs; his wife had often thrown into the swill-bucket more bread than lay on the table now.

'We're hard-up suddenly, ain't we?' he drawled sarcastically.

She was furious. 'It wouldn't worry your head if we were turned into the street, would it?' she flung at him. 'Would it? Would it now?'

Deliberately, with indifference, he put a piece of sausage into his mouth and swallowed it.

'Perhaps you wouldn't understand the difference four people's money can make?' she asked.

Her little red apple-face was burning with indignation. He did not understand it all. He swallowed suddenly.

'What are you driving at?' he asked. 'What d'ye mean—four people?'

She explained it: he had been in prison and the two younger sons had married. She said no more. But he knew suddenly that by the fourth she meant Pauline. This then was the cause of everything; her indignation, the missing sewing-machine, the miserable food, the way she was half-starving him. He reflected bitterly on it all. But inwardly he was sick. He felt crushed. But still he tried hard to preserve the old, flashy manner of indifferent contempt:

'You ain't going to tell me some fine tale about that gal not coming home!'

'I don't know about a fine tale,' said Mrs. Harper. 'But she hasn't come.'

Her voice had lost its quick, indignant tones. Her whole manner was suddenly that of someone worn out, sad, defeated. In his absence she had suffered and in suffering had plainly grown older.

This was the very manner which left him cold. The expression of feminine misery left him dead. He was fundamentally incapable of responding to it. And he struck off at a tangent, angry and blustering again:

'D'ye mean to say you don't know where she is?'

'She's in London.'

'In London? In London? What's she doing *there*, eh?'

'How in the world should I know?'

She spoke slowly, without hope, utterly despondent. He looked at the canary; it had folded itself close and was perching quiet and sleepy, more than ever like some half-awakened lemon bud. The sight of it made him assume at once his favourite attitude. 'A nice thing,' he muttered.

'A nice damn thing!' He liked dearly to imagine himself the victim of some great wrong.

But suddenly his anger burst out even in spite of himself:

'If she ever comes back to this house,' he half-shouted, 'I'll whip the flesh off her!'

'You'll whip the flesh off nothing! Don't belch so much.'

'What?—What?' he threatened. 'And who'll stop me?'

'Never mind who'll stop you. You're too fond of opening your big mouth about that girl. A devil of a lot you did to keep her here when she was here. And a devil of a lot of rest you've lost, I know, worrying about whether she'll ever come back again!'

He jumped to his feet and clapped his hat to his head with a strange mixture of anger and melodramatic ferocity.

'You've whittled enough about her coming back,' he shouted. 'Now whittle about me!'

He was out of the house before she could move or reply. She sat still, worn and scared. A moment later the faintest smile travelled across her lips and her body relaxed again. She knew him perfectly, like a mother. He would come back, perhaps in an hour, perhaps in ten minutes, but she had no doubt at all that he would come.

Nevertheless she was astonished to hear his footsteps again within a minute or two. She was busy turning his shirt on the clothes-horse and she sat down hastily at the scrape of his boot on the stone step outside the door.

And presently, when he came into the room, she was aware instantly of a change in him. She was astounded by his air of misery and defeat: his great body, ordinarily so like a bullock's, bore a look of utter limpness, like a sick child's. When he came and sat down before the fire he looked so abject and unhappily puzzled that she was filled at once with pity.

'What's come over you, man? What's come over you?'

He blinked his eyes and stared. She knew perfectly the sign that he had received some unexpected blow.

'What is it?' she urged.

He looked at her miserably and said:

'Where are the ferrets?'

He spoke slowly, without malice, and she was at once afraid, keeping silent.

'Where are they?' he said. 'The hutches are empty. Not even a mite o' straw.'

He spoke desperately, with alarm and pain, watching her face acutely.

'They're gone,' she said at last. 'They died. It couldn't be helped. It was the frost. It couldn't be helped.'

She waited for him to spring up in anger and half-unconsciously she lifted her hands a little in order to shield her face, but he did not move or speak. Still afraid, she raised the sleeve of his clean shirt and said:

'What about this shirt? Ain't you going to put it on?'

He did not look at her. There was nothing he could say or do against this fresh loss. He was defeated. He could rage and bluster against the girl, the miserable food, the air of snivelling poverty, but the loss of the ferrets struck him like a blow over the heart and left him crushed and speechless.

She moved about timidly, clearing away the supper things. She was afraid to move the canary from the supper-cloth and she let the cage and the cloth remain.

After a little time he thought of Fanny.

'Where is she?' he said.

'She's in bed,' she answered. 'She's had a dragging cold on her chest all winter long.'

'Is she middlin'?' he said.

'I don't know what to make of her. She's for everlasting fretting.'

He looked into the fire and stretched out his hand and fingered his shirt like a man in a dream.

'Everlasting fretting?' he repeated. 'There don't seem to be much right with this house lately.'

'There don't seem to be much right with anything at all,' she said.

CHAPTER XIII

THE boy was sitting once again in the boot-maker's shop with his feet against the stove. It was evening-time; the stove was glowing red and the lamp was alight over the bench by the window. The reflector shone behind the flame like a silver shell and the glow fell upon the bent form of Quintus, hammering industriously. The house-painter was also there, and opposite the boy, on the broken chair where Masher had often sat, another man, very fat and bloated, was sitting in a dignified position, perfectly upright, his left thumb in the arm-hole of his light grey waistcoat. He was dressed in a grey frock-coat with swallow-tails and grey trousers made to a wide, elegant cut; on his head was a bowler hat of the black, square type; his collar was stiff and high and was tied with a white silk muffler frilled and puffed like a stock, and he was wearing long, pointed boots that were the pale yellow colour of tea. His face was enormously large and flabby, his cheeks sagging like the jowls of a pig, but he held his head in a grandiose and dignified way. His eyes were full of a half-humorous, half-aloof expression, but his mouth was hidden by an enormous, drooping moustache that was the colour of tea also. He sat perfectly silent, alternately preening and brushing his moustache in lordly sweeps with the back of his hand and taking snuff in tremendous pinches with a snort like a cow. His name was Push, and he was a bookmaker.

They sat for a time without speaking, Quintus hammering noisily and the boy watching a potato lying in the ashes beneath the stove.

179

Presently Quintus began laughing; he tried at first to control his laughter by hammering more vigorously, but suddenly he threw down his hammer and laughed as if he would choke himself. The boy and the painter stared at him and Push turned his head ever so slightly, with great dignity, almost as if his neck were paralysed with pain, and looked at him too.

'What's the matter with you, Quintus?' he said in a slow, impressive bass. 'What the devil's the matter with you?'

'Ith a blethed fit,' said the painter.

Quintus leaned back and sprawled against the bench and laughed helplessly.

'Christ! if you could have seen him,' he said in a moment. 'If you could have seen him lying on the muck-heap outside the stable trying to say his prayers, and me saying to him, "Get up you dirty bastard, get up you bastard," and every time he dragged himself up me knocking him down again! "And who the hell told you to get up, you bastard?" I'd say to him. "You lay still and comfortable for a bit until you're told to get up!" And there he'd lay. I can see him now, white as a sheet and his apron torn into strips. His lips quivering and blubbering hymns and prayers and God knows what else. And when he'd been laying there a bit I'd stand over him with the whip and say, "Now, lean-guts, get up, you bastard. Get up you bastard!" And then as soon as he got up I'd knock him down again!'

The boy listened with laughter in his face and his heart, and both he and the bookmaker laughed outright while Quintus paused and spat into the stove before going on again:

'I shall never forget it, if I live to be a hundred I shall never forget it,' he said wiping his mouth with his black hand, 'the way I went into that bakehouse after I'd heard

180

about the boy here. When I went in the bakehouse was empty, so I rattled a baking-tin and his old woman came scurrying downstairs fast enough to have a fit. "Mr. Corday about?" I says to her. I never understood that gal. There she is, a fine, strapping woman, wasted on a toad like Corday. I reckon she was dressing for Chapel. She hadn't put a blouse on and I could see her bosom, soft as a bolster. Well, never mind that now. "He's in the stable, Quintus. Will you go along down?" she said. She opened the door for me and I went down the yard. I could hear him in the stable, so I poked my head in at the door and said, "Good-morning, Zachariah!" Zachariah! That's his name! Push, if you had a name like that folks would take you for a bleeding racehorse. Zachariah! Well, Zachariah was grooming the horse a bit and when he heard me say "Zachariah" he jumped as if I'd stuck him with an awl. I never said nothing. I just leaned against the stable door and looked at him. Mind you, I never said a word. And then all of a sudden he looks up and says, "I don't sell bread on Sundays." Bread on Sundays! He didn't sell bread on Sundays! Jesus wept! As if I'd ever choke myself with a bit of his blasted bread again as long as I live. Well, I never said a word. I just leaned against the stable door and looked at him. That's all. And God strike me dead on this bench, Push, if I tell a lie, he went as white as a bloody sheet. He knew what I'd come for. He didn't need no telling. I never see a man turn so white. I went poaching with Ephraim Turner once, Old Buckskin, the night he was shot in the leg. He'd got a rabbit in every one of his pockets and the shot went through his leg just underneath a rabbit's nose. We ran for three miles losing the keepers, and old Buckskin kept saying to me, "I can feel the blood, Quint, I can feel the blood," and I kept telling him it was only the rabbit bleeding down his legs. And when we got home and old Buckskin saw where the shot had hit him he went white, the same, but not half as white as that baker, not half so bloody white. Well, we stood and looked at each other. Mind you, I didn't say a word. And then when I see he didn't need no telling about what I'd come for, I went for him. I knocked him down afore he could open his mouth. Christ, he knew what I'd come for. When he got up again he was blubbing like a woman, but I knocked him down again. And then he got up and rushed at me and I knocked him down again. When I got tired of hitting him I saw the whip. It must have been the same bloody whip the dirty bastard used on the boy here. And Christ, that finished him. I could have killed him, I could have killed him easy while his missus was getting into her best shimmy for chapel. He'd about as much heart as some old ewe. Well, after a bit I made him get up and come into the yard. He staggered about a bit and then fell over a shovel on the muck-heap. And that's where I made him get up and lay down again. "Get up you bastard!" I kept saying to him. "Get up you bastard!" And then as soon as he'd got up I'd knock him down again.'

Quintus broke off and Push and the painter almost fell backwards as they laughed together. At the mention of the whip there had come a repetition of terror and sickness into the boy's heart, but now he too was laughing and as he looked at Quintus the baker seemed a weak, pitiful, inoffensive creature, too weak and ludicrous even to hate now. He stooped to pick up the potato from the ashes and at the same time Quintus, smiting the bench a tremendous blow with the hammer so that all the nails and rivets danced as if with joy, sneered with gleeful contempt: 'I don't sell bread on Sundays. I don't sell bread on Sundays!' The boy felt the heat from the stove on his hands and face, and the potato itself hot in his fingers.

The burning pain in his hand awoke him. He was lying

in bed beside his grandmother and the room was flooded with morning sunlight.

He lay for some moments in a confused state of mind. His eyes revolved sleepily and his brain struggled with the dream of Quintus and the bookmaker in the shop and the actuality of the bright, still room about him. The dream was very real. His heart was still trembling with laughter and he could almost fancy he felt the sharp burning mark of the potato on his fingers, and it was difficult not to believe that he was still by the stove.

When he became fully awake he lay with his hands outside the coverlet and stared at the sky through a narrow strip of the faded brown curtains. The sky was very blue, but the air was sharp and cold, and he wondered what time it could be. For a time there was not a sound and then he heard the lodger's baby whimper softly on the other side of the bedroom wall. Each time he thought of Quintus thrashing the baker he laughed a little to himself, very softly, and the noise of his laughter and of the baby's whimpering were the only sounds.

He half-raised himself in bed and said to his grandmother: 'What time is it?' but the old woman was asleep. She lay like an image of greyish-yellow wax on the white pillow, and though he repeated the words at intervals with soft insistence she did not move or wake.

Sometimes when he had woken before her in the mornings he had leaned over and lifted one of her lids or had wormed his finger into her ear until she opened her eyes.

'You want a 'nation lot of dog pie!' he would say to her.

She often roused him with this expression, which he did not understand, and now he leaned over and whispered it to her and put his fingers gently on the lids of her eyes.

The lids were hard and cold, and as he drew his hand

183

hastily away he touched her cheek and that also was stiff and chilly, like a piece of clay. He was afraid and edged a little away from her. It seemed to him then that her face looked cold and he did not understand this, for the clothes were pulled closely up to her chin, and he leaned over and shook her gently by the shoulders.

Suddenly, when she made no movement or sound to his entreaties but only seemed to grow colder and stiffer, he understood that nothing would ever wake her. The awe of death seized him with a strange, cold terror which acted like something hypnotic upon him. He drew himself away from the old woman until he stood upright by the bed, in his shirt. The room was very still and he was afraid of the stillness and of the unearthly half-light filtering through the curtains on the dead face.

He began to put on his trousers. In the lodger's room the baby began to whimper again, as though it were calling to him, and he suddenly felt also a strange whimpering in his heart. At every button on his trousers he would pause and look at the dead face again, still in the hope that it had changed or moved.

He went downstairs at last and sat in a chair in the kitchen and pulled on his boots. He did everything with a kind of stealthiness, the sight of his grandmother's cold, yellow, immobile face never shifting from his mind. As he drew on his boots he saw lying on a plate on the table a half-eaten sausage and he remembered then that his grandmother had sat there eating the sausage as he went to bed. Instantly the queer thought ran through his mind:

'Perhaps if she could have eaten the sausage she wouldn't have died.'

When he had put on his boots the hypnotic effect of the face on him ceased momentarily, and he was flung into a kind of frightened activity, as if the presence of death were pursuing him. The mere fact of death also

184

would not let him rest and he felt the words 'She is dead! She is dead!' hammering coldly and insistently at the walls of his mind.

He unlocked the door and stepped into the sunshine. The spring air was clear and bright but the sun had no warmth. He walked down the yard and went into the yard where the Harpers lived and there he saw the door was open and he caught the strong odour of bacon being fried. A sensation of hunger mingled with a pang of terror ran down to his bowels.

He went into the kitchen. The bacon was making a strange, spiteful hissing in the pan on the gas-stove. Mrs. Harper was standing over the stove, trying to comb her hair and fry the bacon at the same time.

He stood silent, not knowing how to frame his words.

'What is it?' she said.

Half-absently he watched her thin, greyish hair run through the comb. He felt paralysed with fear and there was a choking sound in his throat as he tried to answer her. He remained so strangely dumb that she had to repeat her words, and only then could he say:

'Granny won't wake. She won't wake. Go and look at her. I can't wake her.'

'What have you done?' She turned out the gas-jet under the frying-pan.

'I shook her but she won't wake.'

She turned pale. He saw her fingers trembling as she tried to twist up the skein of hair. For an unconscionable time she tried to make her quivering fingers fix the knot of hair in its place. She tried to hold the hair-pins in her mouth but her lips faltered apart and the pins fell tinkling to the floor. The boy fell on his knees but she ran to the door without heeding him, the hair tumbling untidily down her neck again. Before he could rise to his feet he heard her scuffling back. He saw her run into the living-room and wrench open the door and call in a desperate voice:

'Get up my darling, quick! Quick! There's a cup of tea on the table for you! Get up for God's sake!'

He felt at once that she had gone mad. Without speaking to him again she ran out of the house and vanished. He rose to his feet and went into the living-room and stood quite still, not knowing what to do.

The room was empty and the canary-cage, not yet uncovered, was hanging motionless from its white-washed hook in the ceiling by the window. The green cloth with the golden harp had been pinned about it by a large yellow safety-pin. The window-blind, drawn up hastily, was hanging crookedly, and the pale vapour from the cup of tea standing on the table was vanishing thinly upwards in the sunshine pouring in beneath the blind.

There was not a sound. He stood still, trying to gather his thoughts. His boots were still unlaced and the straps of his braces were twisted and uncomfortable and his eyes were still drooping and clogged with sleep. His thoughts were not very quick or sad. There was only a sensation of coldness in his heart. His grandmother was dead and nothing could recall her. Nothing could change or spirit away that unearthly yellow expression of death from her face.

It seemed to him that he stood there for a long time in silence before he heard the sound of footsteps in the room above him and then on the wooden stairs as they began slowly to come down. The footsteps were soft and shuffling and he was conscious, at the sound of them, of his heart beginning to beat with faster and heavier beats again.

When the footsteps ceased at last there was a faint cough and he looked at the door. He looked as though spellbound.

He was standing face to face with Pauline.

The sight of her seemed to strike his senses with that same wild, incredible swiftness as when the whip had curled over his back in the dark stable. He stood as if stupefied. He could not move or speak.

She too stood still. He looked at her mechanically and began to take in the details of her face, its dead paleness, the sombre eyes, the startled expression, the faint parting of the lips as though she were about to speak to him. She had dressed hastily. Her dress was crumpled and the bodice had not been evenly fastened, so that the opening of the neck had slipped askew, showing the clear whiteness of her shoulder. It was an old dark-green dress with the sleeves and collar of white lace. He had seen it many times before. She came forward and stood on the hearth-rug. He caught the word 'Adam,' uttered with soft astonishment. She looked like someone who had dressed hastily after a long journey. She smiled and gazed at his dishevelled, half-dressed appearance and seemed to recollect something.

'Why did my mother shout like that?' she said. 'Where is she?'

'She's gone to look at my grandmother,' he answered.

'Your grandmother?' she said. 'What's the matter with her? What's the matter with your grandmother?'

He told her quickly.

'She died in the night. While I was asleep,' he added.

He heard her lips repeat his name a second time. Her voice was pained, uncertain, incredulous. She looked at him with compassion and for one moment he was afraid that she would embrace him. But to his relief she stood still and was silent, nothing except the motion of her rising and falling breast breaking up the immobility of her body.

For what seemed a long time they stood silent. He was inexpressibly glad that she was silent. She understood and he felt her understanding. There could be no doubt of her compassion. By her very silence he felt that she was suffering.

She broke the silence at last by saying:

'Come here to me. Your braces are so twisted.'

He went to her quietly and obediently and stood facing the window. The tea was growing cold. The canary was beginning to flutter against the cage. Pauline knelt down behind the boy. He felt her fingers running over the straps of his braces and pressing them straight and smooth as ribbons once more.

While she was kneeling down busy with the buttons, he said in a low voice:

'When did you come back again?'

She did not lift her head.

'A week ago.'

'I never knew you'd come,' he said.

She gave the buttons skilful little twists with her fingers. They snapped into place.

'I've been ill since then,' she said.

She ran her hands quickly over his chest and smoothed his shirt. Her black hair, shot with many dull emerald lights, like the gleam of a rook's wing, gleamed bright and smooth in the strong sunshine. The parting was pencilled white and straight. The tenderness of her hands as they ran over his chest seemed to electrify him. He caught the faint scent of her dress, the soft heat of her bosom, the mysterious, intangible fragrance of femininity about her. And for a moment he felt an overpowering desire to say to her, 'Where have you been? Where's Masher? Why did you come back again?' But the mere fact of her presence, combined with a moment of terror as he recalled the yellow image and the dead face of his grandmother lying beside him in the bed, seemed to stupefy him as those last blows of the baker's whip had done. He said nothing and in another moment she got to her feet. He felt pleasant and comfortable about his shoulders now, but the silence itself he could bear no longer.

'Uncover the canary,' he said.

As he spoke there were suddenly sounds overhead of someone getting up, a blind snapped up with a sharp grating of rollers, a voice coughing gutturally and spitting with great sighs. A moment later came the voice of Quintus:

'Pauline! Pauline!'

She went to the foot of the stairs and said quietly:

'Yes, I'm here.'

'Get us a bit of sausage for breakfast!'

'Where do you think I can get sausage?' she said, 'at this time of day!'

'Who's down there?' he called.

She told him.

'Can't you send him for a mite?' he said.

She did not answer and there was a little silence before he shouted back:

'What's the matter with you. Don't he want to go?'

'Where do you think he can go?' she said.

'Can't he go to Jonathan's? He'll get it on tick. He can say it's for his old grandmother.'

She turned away from the foot of the stairs and came to where the boy was standing white and motionless under the canary-cage and said:

'Will you go?'

He nodded his head almost mechanically, without a word. Her face was deadly pale. She turned away and opened a drawer in the table and took out a black purse and put a shilling in his hand. Her hands were slow and unsteady, like an old woman's. It seemed as if she would never do up the silver clasp of the purse again.

'Will he go?' Quintus shouted.

'He'll go,' she answered.

189

'Drink a mouthful of tea before you go,' she said to the boy.

She picked up the cup of tea. The surface of the tea trembled and the cup ran over. He drank. The tea was almost cold and the taste of it flat and unpleasant and bitter. When he had finished drinking she took the cup and drank also and they drank alternately until the cup was empty.

The girl was the last to drink. Adam waited for her to drain the cup. He watched the agitation and the rippling of her white throat, tilted slightly backward in the sunshine. She seemed to drink for a long time. He felt the rim of the shilling grow harsh against the palm of his hand and in the silence the ticking of the clock on the mantelpiece seemed to grow louder.

Finally the girl lowered the empty cup to its saucer again. He waited. She did not speak. Suddenly Quintus bellowed:

'God Almighty, ain't that boy gone?'

She gave one swift glance at the boy. Instantly he started as though in terror, went to the door and vanished. She raised her voice a fraction and called:

'Yes, he's gone.'

The clatter of the boy's boots in the yard died away. The canary fluttered behind the green-and-gold canopy, brushed its wings against the wires, chirped thinly and came to rest. The room was silent, as though nothing had happened.

A moment later the girl sat down, shut her eyes, and covered her face with her hands.

THE END

FOR THE BEST IN PAPERBACKS, LOOK FOR THE

In every corner of the world, on every subject under the sun, Penguin represents quality and variety – the very best in publishing today.

For complete information about books available from Penguin – including Pelicans, Puffins, Peregrines and Penguin Classics – and how to order them, write to us at the appropriate address below. Please note that for copyright reasons the selection of books varies from country to country.

In the United Kingdom: For a complete list of books available from Penguin in the U.K., please write to *Dept E.P., Penguin Books Ltd, Harmondsworth, Middlesex, UB7 0DA*

In the United States: For a complete list of books available from Penguin in the U.S., please write to *Dept BA, Penguin, 299 Murray Hill Parkway, East Rutherford, New Jersey 07073*

In Canada: For a complete list of books available from Penguin in Canada, please write to *Penguin Books Canada Ltd, 2801 John Street, Markham, Ontario L3R 1B4*

In Australia: For a complete list of books available from Penguin in Australia, please write to the *Marketing Department, Penguin Books Australia Ltd, P.O. Box 257, Ringwood, Victoria 3134*

In New Zealand: For a complete list of books available from Penguin in New Zealand, please write to the *Marketing Department, Penguin Books (NZ) Ltd, Private Bag, Takapuna, Auckland 9*

In India: For a complete list of books available from Penguin, please write to *Penguin Overseas Ltd, 706 Eros Apartments, 56 Nehru Place, New Delhi, 110019*

In Holland: For a complete list of books available from Penguin in Holland, please write to *Penguin Books Nederland B.V., Postbus 195, NL–1380AD Weesp, Netherlands*

In Germany: For a complete list of books available from Penguin, please write to *Penguin Books Ltd, Friedrichstrasse 10 – 12, D–6000 Frankfurt Main 1, Federal Republic of Germany*

In Spain: For a complete list of books available from Penguin in Spain, please write to *Longman Penguin España, Calle San Nicolas 15, E–28013 Madrid, Spain*

A selection of H. E. Bates in Penguin

FAIR STOOD THE WIND FOR FRANCE

'*Fair Stood the Wind for France* is perhaps the finest novel of the war ... The scenes are exquisitely done and the characters – tenderly and beautifully drawn – are an epitome of all that is best in the youth of the two countries. This is a fine, lovely book which makes the heart beat with pride' – *Daily Telegraph*

THE TRIPLE ECHO

H. E. Bates tells movingly the strange tale of a lonely woman and her love affair with a young deserter, of their intrigues and their deceptions and the elaborate web they weave to outwit the Military Police.

LOVE FOR LYDIA

'Bates at his best ... I read the tale with a sense of eager dread, so real are these folk, so torn and buffeted, and finally so humbled under the winds of passion and the even more terrifying peace which comes when the storm is over ... A book likely to be one of the most-read love stories of our time' – Richard Church

THE WILD CHERRY TREE

These ten stories show Bates at his most tense and immediate; observing with baleful accuracy just what happens when people are 'thrown suddenly with neither direction nor compass into territory utterly strange and unexplored'.